How to Use This Book

Everything you need to know about
Pokémon can be found here in this
comprehensive two-volume guide.

This is volume 2 of 2!

The Pokémon in this book are presented in
their National Pokédex order. This volume
contains numbers 246 to 491, Larvitar to
Darkrai. Volume 1 contains numbers 001
to 245, Bulbasaur to Suicune.

If you would like to look up a Pokémon by
name, there is an alphabetical index at the
end of both volumes.

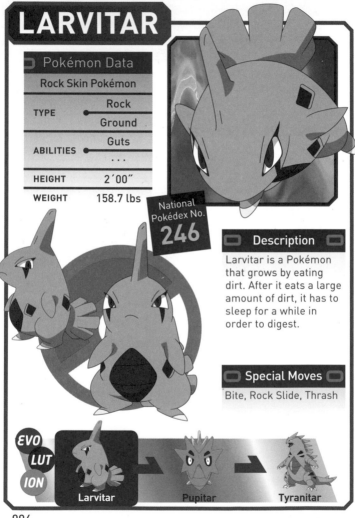

LARVITAR

Pokémon Data

Rock Skin Pokémon

TYPE	Rock
	Ground
ABILITIES	Guts
	...
HEIGHT	2´00″
WEIGHT	158.7 lbs

National Pokédex No.
246

Description

Larvitar is a Pokémon that grows by eating dirt. After it eats a large amount of dirt, it has to sleep for a while in order to digest.

Special Moves

Bite, Rock Slide, Thrash

EVO LUT ION

Larvitar → Pupitar → Tyranitar

PUPITAR

Pokémon Data

Hard Shell Pokémon

TYPE	Rock
	Ground
ABILITIES	Shed Skin
	. . .
HEIGHT	3′11″
WEIGHT	335.1 lbs

National Pokédex No.
247

Description

Although Pupitar's body is surrounded by a rock-hard shell, it can move around easily by venting pressurized gas like a rocket.

Special Moves

Screech, Scary Face, Dark Pulse

EVO LUT ION

Larvitar → Pupitar → Tyranitar

1-49
50-99
100-149
150-199
200-249
250-299
300-349
350-399
400-449
450-491

TYRANITAR

Pokémon Data

Armor Pokémon

TYPE	Rock
	Dark
ABILITIES	Sand Stream
	. . .
HEIGHT	6'07"
WEIGHT	445.3 lbs

National Pokédex No.
248

Description

Tyranitar's body is impervious to nearly any kind of attack. When it goes on a rampage, mountains crumble and rivers are filled in. Every time this happens maps have to be redrawn.

Special Moves

Stone Edge, Hyper Beam, Crunch, Earthquake

EVOLUTION

Larvitar → Pupitar → Tyranitar

LUGIA

Pokémon Data

Diving Pokémon

TYPE	Psychic
	Flying
ABILITIES	Pressure
	. . .
HEIGHT	17´01˝
WEIGHT	476.2 lbs

National Pokédex No.
249

Description

A Legendary Pokémon called "The Guardian of the Sea," Lugia lies sleeping at the bottom of the ocean. When it rouses and flies, the flapping of its wings causes storms that last for forty days.

Special Moves

Hydro Pump, Aeroblast, Calm Mind

EVO LUT ION

Lugia

Does not Evolve

49
50-99
100-149
150-199
200-249
250-299
300-349
350-399
400-449
450-491

HO-OH

Pokémon Data

Rainbow Pokémon

TYPE	Fire
	Flying
ABILITIES	Pressure
	...
HEIGHT	12´06˝
WEIGHT	438.7 lbs

Description

A Legendary Pokémon, Ho-Oh flies about the world on rainbow-colored wings. Those who gaze upon it are said to be blessed with happiness.

National Pokédex No.

250

Special Moves

Fire Blast, Sacred Fire, Sky Attack

EVOLUTION

Ho-Oh

Does not Evolve

CELEBI

Pokémon Data

Time Travel Pokémon

TYPE	Psychic
	Grass
ABILITIES	Natural Cure
	. . .
HEIGHT	2′00″
WEIGHT	11.0 lbs

Description

Celebi has the power to travel through time, but it only appears during peaceful periods. In the forest where Celebi disappeared, it left behind an Egg it brought from the future.

National Pokédex No.
251

Special Moves

Confusion, Future Sight, Leaf Storm

EVOLUTION

Celebi

Does not Evolve

1-49
50-99
100-149
150-199
200-249
250-299
300-349
350-399
400-449
450-491

TREECKO

Pokémon Data

Wood Gecko Pokémon

TYPE	Grass ...
ABILITIES	Overgrow ...
HEIGHT	1´08˝
WEIGHT	11.0 lbs

National Pokédex No.
252

Description

It can climb up steep walls thanks to the tiny spikes on the bottoms of its feet. Even when being challenged by an opponent far greater in size, Treecko will not back down.

Special Moves

Absorb, Quick Attack, Pursuit

EVOLUTION

Treecko → Grovyle → Sceptile

GROVYLE

Pokémon Data

Wood Gecko Pokémon

TYPE	Grass …
ABILITIES	Overgrow …
HEIGHT	2′11″
WEIGHT	47.6 lbs

1-49
50-99
100-149
150-199
200-249
250-299
300-349
350-399
400-449
450-491

Description

Grovyle lives mostly in forests and is skilled at climbing trees. It stalks its prey by jumping from branch to branch. The leaves on its body are useful for camouflaging itself.

Special Moves

Absorb, Leaf Blade, Agility

National Pokédex No.
253

EVO LUT ION

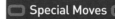

Treecko

Grovyle

Sceptile

SCEPTILE

Pokémon Data

Forest Pokémon

TYPE	Grass . . .
ABILITIES	Overgrow . . .
HEIGHT	5´07˝
WEIGHT	115.1 lbs

National Pokédex No.
254

Description

Sceptile takes good care of the trees of the forest. The seeds on its back are stuffed with nutrients that energize trees. The leaves on its arms are very sharp and strong.

Special Moves

Slam, False Swipe, Leaf Storm

EVOLUTION

Treecko → Grovyle → Sceptile

TORCHIC

Pokémon Data

Chick Pokémon

TYPE	Fire ...
ABILITIES	Blaze ...
HEIGHT	1´04˝
WEIGHT	5.5 lbs

Description

If Torchic is attacked, it will shoot out a fireball with a temperature of over 1,800°F. Because there's a fire burning in its body, it feels warm when you hug it.

Special Moves

Scratch, Ember, Peck, Sand Attack

National Pokédex No.
255

EVO LUT ION

Torchic → Combusken → Blaziken

1-49
50-99
100-149
150-199
200-249
250-299
300-349
350-399
400-449
450-491

COMBUSKEN

Pokémon Data

Young Fowl Pokémon

TYPE	Fire
	Fighting
ABILITIES	Blaze
	. . .
HEIGHT	2´11˝
WEIGHT	43.0 lbs

National Pokédex No.
256

Description

Combusken fights by blasting blazing-hot flames from its beak, and it can unleash ten lightning-fast kicks a second. It keeps its legs in shape by running through hills and fields.

Special Moves

Double Kick, Bulk Up, Quick Attack

EVOLUTION

Torchic → Combusken → Blaziken

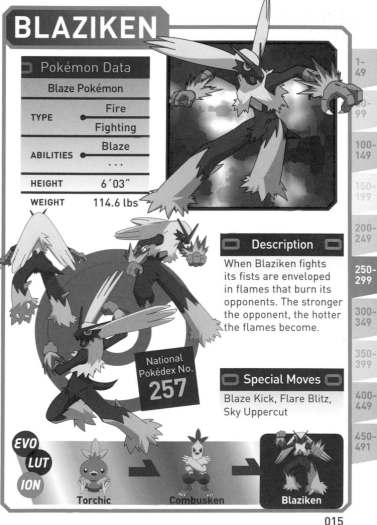

BLAZIKEN

Pokémon Data

Blaze Pokémon

TYPE	Fire
	Fighting
ABILITIES	Blaze
	. . .
HEIGHT	6´03"
WEIGHT	114.6 lbs

National Pokédex No.
257

Description

When Blaziken fights its fists are enveloped in flames that burn its opponents. The stronger the opponent, the hotter the flames become.

Special Moves

Blaze Kick, Flare Blitz, Sky Uppercut

EVO LUT ION

Torchic → Combusken → Blaziken

1–49
50–99
100–149
150–199
200–249
250–299
300–349
350–399
400–449
450–491

MUDKIP

Pokémon Data

Mud Fish Pokémon

TYPE	Water
	. . .
ABILITIES	Torrent
	. . .
HEIGHT	1´04˝
WEIGHT	16.8 lbs

National Pokédex No.
258

Description

Mudkip detects changes in the flow of the surrounding air and water through the fin on its head. It breathes underwater using the gills on its cheeks.

Special Moves

Growl, Mud-Slap, Water Gun, Tackle

EVOLUTION

Mudkip → Marshtomp → Swampert

MARSHTOMP

Pokémon Data

Mud Fish Pokémon

TYPE	Water
	Ground
ABILITIES	Torrent
	. . .
HEIGHT	2´04"
WEIGHT	61.7 lbs

1-
49

50-
99

100-
149

150-
199

200-
249

250-
299

300-
349

350-
399

400-
449

450-
491

Description

Marshtomp has adjusted to living on land by covering its entire body with a thin, protective layer of slime. It can walk easily even on marshy ground thanks to its adapted feet.

National Pokédex No.
259

Special Moves

Mud Shot, Take Down, Muddy Water

EVO LUT ION

Mudkip ➡ Marshtomp ➡ Swampert

SWAMPERT

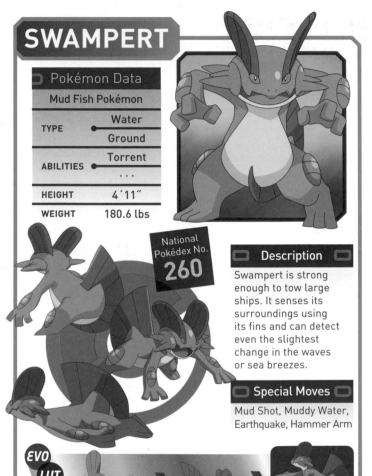

Pokémon Data

Mud Fish Pokémon

TYPE	Water
	Ground
ABILITIES	Torrent
	. . .
HEIGHT	4´11″
WEIGHT	180.6 lbs

National Pokédex No.
260

Description

Swampert is strong enough to tow large ships. It senses its surroundings using its fins and can detect even the slightest change in the waves or sea breezes.

Special Moves

Mud Shot, Muddy Water, Earthquake, Hammer Arm

EVO LUT ION

Mudkip ▶ Marshtomp ▶ Swampert

POOCHYENA

Pokémon Data

Bite Pokémon

TYPE	Dark
	. . .
ABILITIES	Run Away
	Quick Feet
HEIGHT	1´08″
WEIGHT	30.0 lbs

National Pokédex No.

261

Description

The size of Poochyena's fangs is large relative to its body. It can eat pretty much anything. It will agressively pursue its prey, but if the prey fights back it can be scared off.

Special Moves

Howl, Bite, Tackle

EVOLUTION

Poochyena → Mightyena

50-99

100-149

150-199

200-249

250-299

300-349

350-399

400-449

450-491

MIGHTYENA

Pokémon Data

Bite Pokémon

TYPE	Dark
	...
ABILITIES	Intimidate
	Quick Feet
HEIGHT	3´03″
WEIGHT	81.06 lbs

Description

Mightyena howls and crouches low right before springing into its attack. It will never disobey a Trainer it deems to be its leader.

Special Moves

Assurance, Taunt, Take Down, Sucker Punch

National Pokédex No.
262

EVO
LUT
ION

Poochyena → Mightyena

ZIGZAGOON

Pokémon Data

Tiny Raccoon Pokémon

TYPE	Normal
	. . .
ABILITIES	Pickup
	Gluttony
HEIGHT	1′04″
WEIGHT	38.6 lbs

National Pokédex No.
263

1–49
50–79
100–149
150–199
200–249
250–299
300–349
350–399
400–449
450–491

Description

Zigzagoon is interested in so many things that it ends up walking in a zigzag manner. It's skilled at finding things in the grass or even treasure buried underground.

Special Moves

Sand Attack, Odor Sleuth, Tail Whip, Headbutt

EVO LUT ION

Zigzagoon → Linoone

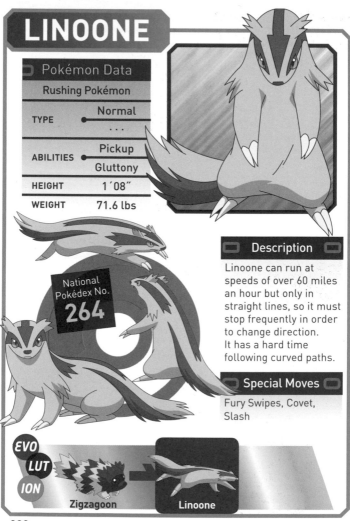

LINOONE

Pokémon Data

Rushing Pokémon

TYPE	Normal
	. . .
ABILITIES	Pickup
	Gluttony
HEIGHT	1´08˝
WEIGHT	71.6 lbs

National Pokédex No.
264

Description

Linoone can run at speeds of over 60 miles an hour but only in straight lines, so it must stop frequently in order to change direction. It has a hard time following curved paths.

Special Moves

Fury Swipes, Covet, Slash

EVO LUT ION

Zigzagoon → Linoone

1-
49

50-
99

100-
149

150-
199

200-
249

250-
299

300-
349

350-
399

400-
449

450-
491

WURMPLE

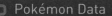

Pokémon Data

Worm Pokémon

TYPE	Bug
	. . .
ABILITIES	Shield Dust
	. . .
HEIGHT	1´00˝
WEIGHT	7.9 lbs

National
Pokédex No.
265

Description

If attacked, Wurmple fights back using the spikes on its tail, weakening its enemies with poison. It can also immobilize them with the silk spewed from its mouth.

Special Moves

Tackle, String Shot, Poison Sting

**EVO
LUT
ION**

Wurmple

Silcoon

Cascoon

Beautifly

Dustox

023

SILCOON

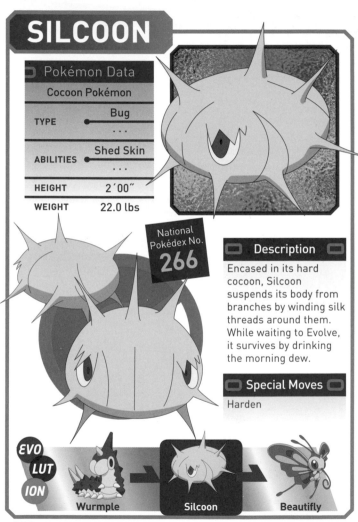

Pokémon Data

Cocoon Pokémon

TYPE	Bug
	...
ABILITIES	Shed Skin
	...
HEIGHT	2´00˝
WEIGHT	22.0 lbs

National Pokédex No.
266

Description

Encased in its hard cocoon, Silcoon suspends its body from branches by winding silk threads around them. While waiting to Evolve, it survives by drinking the morning dew.

Special Moves

Harden

EVO LUT ION

Wurmple ▶ Silcoon ▶ Beautifly

BEAUTIFLY

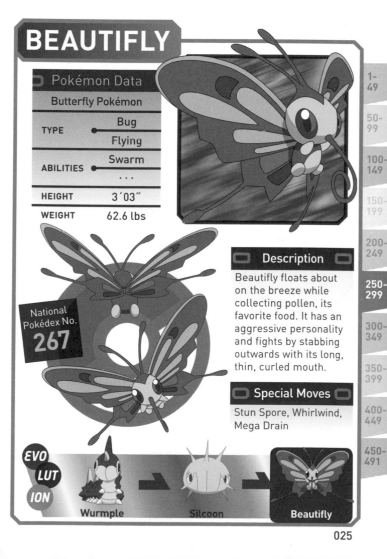

Pokémon Data

Butterfly Pokémon

TYPE	Bug
	Flying
ABILITIES	Swarm
	. . .
HEIGHT	3′03″
WEIGHT	62.6 lbs

National Pokédex No.

267

Description

Beautifly floats about on the breeze while collecting pollen, its favorite food. It has an aggressive personality and fights by stabbing outwards with its long, thin, curled mouth.

Special Moves

Stun Spore, Whirlwind, Mega Drain

EVO LUT ION

Wurmple ➜ Silcoon ➜ Beautifly

1-49
50-99
100-149
150-199
200-249
250-299
300-349
350-399
400-449
450-491

CASCOON

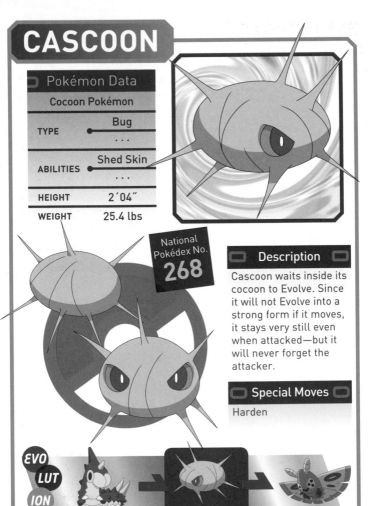

Pokémon Data

Cocoon Pokémon

TYPE	Bug
	...
ABILITIES	Shed Skin
	...
HEIGHT	2´04˝
WEIGHT	25.4 lbs

National Pokédex No.
268

Description

Cascoon waits inside its cocoon to Evolve. Since it will not Evolve into a strong form if it moves, it stays very still even when attacked—but it will never forget the attacker.

Special Moves

Harden

EVOLUTION

Wurmple → Cascoon → Dustox

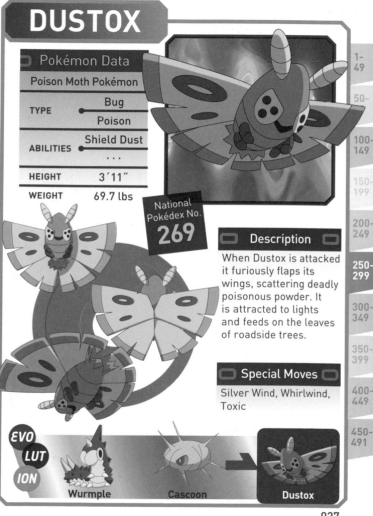

DUSTOX

Pokémon Data

Poison Moth Pokémon

TYPE	Bug
	Poison
ABILITIES	Shield Dust
	. . .
HEIGHT	3´11″
WEIGHT	69.7 lbs

National Pokédex No.
269

1-
49

50-

100-
149

150-
199

200-
249

250-
299

300-
349

350-
399

400-
449

450-
491

Description

When Dustox is attacked it furiously flaps its wings, scattering deadly poisonous powder. It is attracted to lights and feeds on the leaves of roadside trees.

Special Moves

Silver Wind, Whirlwind, Toxic

EVO LUT ION

Wurmple → Cascoon → Dustox

027

LOTAD

Pokémon Data

Water Weed Pokémon

TYPE	Water
	Grass
ABILITIES	Swift Swim
	Rain Dish
HEIGHT	1´08″
WEIGHT	5.7 lbs

National Pokédex No.
270

Description

Lotad floats on the surface of ponds and lakes. It becomes weak if the leaf on top of its head dries out. It can ferry small Pokémon that cannot swim across the water.

Special Moves

Absorb, Nature Power, Growl

EVO LUT ION

Lotad

Lombre

Ludicolo

LOMBRE

Pokémon Data

Jolly Pokémon

TYPE	Water
	Grass
ABILITIES	Swift Swim
	Rain Dish
HEIGHT	3'11"
WEIGHT	71.6 lbs

Description

Lombre becomes more active when the sun goes down. When it spots someone fishing it will mischievously tug on the line from under the water.

National Pokédex No.
271

Special Moves

Fury Swipes, Water Sport, Zen Headbutt

EVO LUT ION

Lotad → Lombre → Ludicolo

1-9
50-99
100-149
150-199
200-249
250-299
300-349
350-399
400-449
450-491

LUDICOLO

Pokémon Data

Carefree Pokémon

TYPE	Water
	Grass
ABILITIES	Swift Swim
	Rain Dish
HEIGHT	4´11″
WEIGHT	121.3 lbs

Description

Whenever Ludicolo hears lively music it becomes energized and starts to dance. It can't help itself: the rhythm of the music makes its body move.

Special Moves

Astonish, Mega Drain, Nature Power

National Pokédex No.
272

EVO LUT ION

Lotad → Lombre → Ludicolo

SEEDOT

Pokémon Data

Acorn Pokémon

TYPE	Grass
	. . .
ABILITIES	Chlorophyll
	Early Bird
HEIGHT	1´08˝
WEIGHT	8.8 lbs

National Pokédex No.
273

1–49
50–99
100–149
150–199
200–249
250–299
300–349
350–399
400–449
450–491

Description

Seedot hangs from branches by the top of its head. When it does so it looks just like a nut; it likes surprising other Pokémon that mistake it for food.

Special Moves

Harden, Growth, Synthesis

EVO LUT ION

Seedot → Nuzleaf → Shiftry

NUZLEAF

Pokémon Data

	Wily Pokémon
TYPE	Grass
	Dark
ABILITIES	Chlorophyll
	Early Bird
HEIGHT	3´03˝
WEIGHT	61.7 lbs

Description

Nuzleaf lives deep within the forest and from time to time comes out to startle humans. The sound of its leaf whistle makes those lost in the forest uneasy.

Special Moves

Razor Leaf, Torment, Feint Attack

National Pokédex No.
274

EVO LUT ION

Seedot → Nuzleaf → Shiftry

SHIFTRY

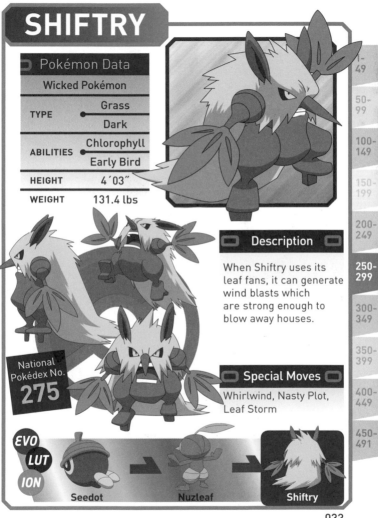

Pokémon Data

Wicked Pokémon

| TYPE | Grass |
| | Dark |

| ABILITIES | Chlorophyll |
| | Early Bird |

| HEIGHT | 4'03" |
| WEIGHT | 131.4 lbs |

Description

When Shiftry uses its leaf fans, it can generate wind blasts which are strong enough to blow away houses.

Special Moves

Whirlwind, Nasty Plot, Leaf Storm

National Pokédex No.
275

EVO LUT ION

Seedot → Nuzleaf → Shiftry

1-49
50-99
100-149
150-199
200-249
250-299
300-349
350-399
400-449
450-491

TAILLOW

Pokémon Data

Tiny Swallow Pokémon

TYPE	Normal
	Flying
ABILITIES	Guts
	. . .
HEIGHT	1´00˝
WEIGHT	5.1 lbs

National Pokédex No.
276

Description

Taillow migrates in search of warm lands. It bravely confronts powerful opponents, but when it gets hungry or lonely during the night, it cries loudly.

Special Moves

Quick Attack, Wing Attack, Endeavor

EVO LUT ION

Taillow → Swellow

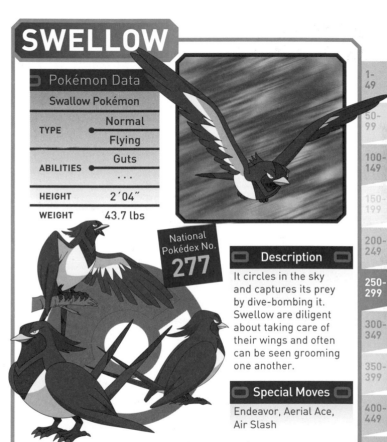

SWELLOW

Pokémon Data

Swallow Pokémon

TYPE	Normal
	Flying

ABILITIES	Guts
	. . .

HEIGHT	2´04″
WEIGHT	43.7 lbs

National Pokédex No.
277

1-49
50-99
100-149
150-199
200-249
250-299
300-349
350-399
400-449
450-491

Description

It circles in the sky and captures its prey by dive-bombing it. Swellow are diligent about taking care of their wings and often can be seen grooming one another.

Special Moves

Endeavor, Aerial Ace, Air Slash

EVOLUTION

Taillow → Swellow

WINGULL

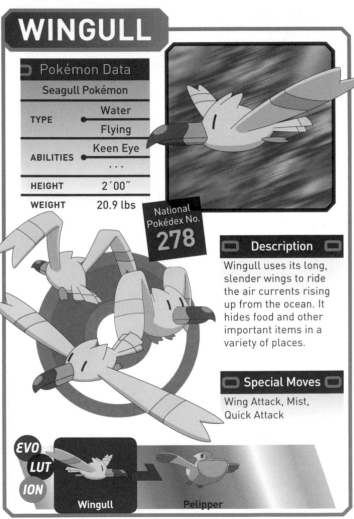

Pokémon Data

Seagull Pokémon

TYPE	Water
	Flying
ABILITIES	Keen Eye
	...
HEIGHT	2′00″
WEIGHT	20.9 lbs

National Pokédex No.
278

Description

Wingull uses its long, slender wings to ride the air currents rising up from the ocean. It hides food and other important items in a variety of places.

Special Moves

Wing Attack, Mist, Quick Attack

EVOLUTION

Wingull → Pelipper

PELIPPER

Pokémon Data

Water Bird Pokémon

TYPE	Water
	Flying
ABILITIES	Keen Eye
	. . .
HEIGHT	3´11″
WEIGHT	61.7 lbs

1-
49

50-
99

100-
149

150-
199

200-
249

250-
299

300-
349

350-
399

400-
449

450-
491

Description

Pelipper can carry Eggs or small Pokémon in its mouth. It flies low over the ocean waves, and when it finds food it scoops it up out of the water in one motion.

National Pokédex No. **279**

Special Moves

Protect, Stockpile, Swallow, Spit Up

EVOLUTION

Wingull → Pelipper

037

RALTS

Pokémon Data

Feeling Pokémon

TYPE	Psychic ...
ABILITIES	Synchronize Trace
HEIGHT	1′04″
WEIGHT	14.6 lbs

Description

Ralts can sense human emotions through the crests on its head. It likes to be around people with positive feelings. When its Trainer is happy, it's happy too.

Special Moves

Confusion, Lucky Chant, Growl, Teleport

EVOLUTION

Ralts

Kirlia

Gallade

Gardevoir

KIRLIA

Pokémon Data

Emotion Pokémon

TYPE	Psychic …
ABILITIES	Synchronize Trace
HEIGHT	2'07"
WEIGHT	44.5 lbs

National Pokédex No.
281

Description

Kirlia can sense what its Trainer is feeling. Because of its highly Evolved mind it can manipulate psychic energy. It dances when it's happy.

Special Moves

Calm Mind, Psychic, Future Sight

EVO LUT ION

Ralts → **Kirlia** → Gallade Gardevoir

1-49
50-99
100-149
150-199
200-249
250-299
300-349
350-399
400-449
450-491

GARDEVOIR

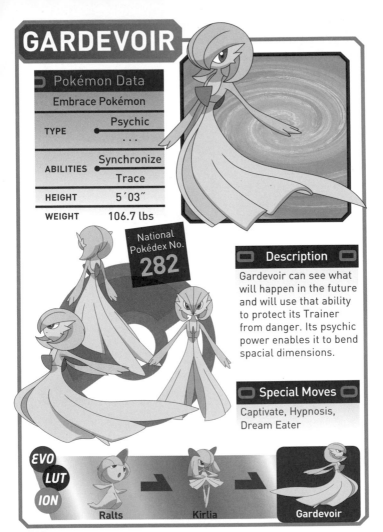

Pokémon Data

Embrace Pokémon

TYPE	Psychic . . .
ABILITIES	Synchronize Trace
HEIGHT	5´03˝
WEIGHT	106.7 lbs

National Pokédex No.
282

Description

Gardevoir can see what will happen in the future and will use that ability to protect its Trainer from danger. Its psychic power enables it to bend spatial dimensions.

Special Moves

Captivate, Hypnosis, Dream Eater

EVOLUTION

Ralts → Kirlia → Gardevoir

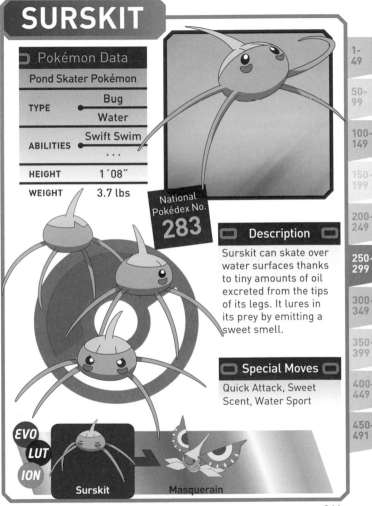

SURSKIT

Pokémon Data

Pond Skater Pokémon

TYPE	Bug
	Water
ABILITIES	Swift Swim
	. . .
HEIGHT	1´08˝
WEIGHT	3.7 lbs

National Pokédex No.
283

1-49
50-99
100-149
150-199
200-249
250-299
300-349
350-399
400-449
450-491

Description

Surskit can skate over water surfaces thanks to tiny amounts of oil excreted from the tips of its legs. It lures in its prey by emitting a sweet smell.

Special Moves

Quick Attack, Sweet Scent, Water Sport

EVO LUT ION

Surskit → Masquerain

MASQUERAIN

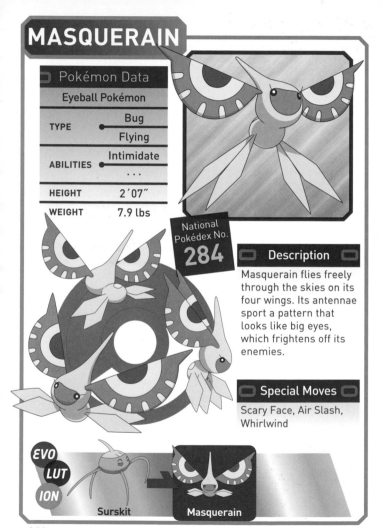

Pokémon Data

Eyeball Pokémon

TYPE	Bug
	Flying
ABILITIES	Intimidate
	...
HEIGHT	2´07˝
WEIGHT	7.9 lbs

National Pokédex No.
284

Description

Masquerain flies freely through the skies on its four wings. Its antennae sport a pattern that looks like big eyes, which frightens off its enemies.

Special Moves

Scary Face, Air Slash, Whirlwind

EVOLUTION

Surskit → Masquerain

SHROOMISH

Pokémon Data

Mushroom Pokémon

TYPE	Grass
	...

ABILITIES	Effect Spore
	Poison Heal
HEIGHT	1´04˝
WEIGHT	9.9 lbs

1–
49

50–
99

100–
149

150–
199

200–
249

250–
299

300–
349

350–
399

400–
449

450–
491

Description

Shroomish lives in wet, and damp locations deep within the forest. When it senses danger it shoots poisonous spores from the top of its head that are strong enough to wilt grass.

Special Moves

Stun Spore, Leech Seed, Mega Drain

National Pokédex No.
285

EVO LUT ION

Shroomish   Breloom

BRELOOM

Pokémon Data

Mushroom Pokémon

TYPE	Grass
	Fighting
ABILITIES	Effect Spore
	Poison Heal
HEIGHT	3'11"
WEIGHT	86.4 lbs

National Pokédex No.
286

Description

Breloom gets in close to its opponent before stretching out its short arms to throw a punch. There are poisonous spores on the tip of its tail.

Special Moves

Mach Punch, Mind Reader, Seed Bomb

EVO LUT ION

Shroomish → Breloom

SLAKOTH

Pokémon Data

Slacker Pokémon

TYPE • Normal
. . .

ABILITIES • Truant
. . .

HEIGHT 2´07˝

WEIGHT 52.9 lbs

National Pokédex No.
287

Description

Slakoth lies around sleeping for over twenty hours a day. It hardly moves at all, and all it eats are three leaves a day. Just looking at it can make you sleepy.

Special Moves

Yawn, Encore, Slack Off, Feint Attack

EVO LUT ION

Slakoth → Vigoroth → Slaking

1-49
50-99
100-149
150-199
200-249
250-299
300-349
350-399
400-449
450-491

VIGOROTH

Pokémon Data

Wild Monkey Pokémon

TYPE	Normal
	. . .
ABILITIES	Vital Spirit
	. . .
HEIGHT	4´07″
WEIGHT	102.5 lbs

Description

Vigoroth has such a fast metabolism that it can't stay still for long. If it doesn't move enough it gets too stressed to sleep at night. Because of this, Vigoroth are always dashing around.

National Pokédex No.

288

Special Moves

Fury Swipes, Focus Punch, Slash, Reversal

EVOLUTION

Slakoth → Vigoroth → Slaking

SLAKING

Pokémon Data

Lazy Pokémon

| TYPE | Normal |
| | ... |

| ABILITIES | Truant |
| | ... |

| HEIGHT | 6´07" |
| WEIGHT | 287.7 lbs |

National Pokédex No.
289

Description

Slaking spends the entire day lounging around and eating grass. It seems that it's the world's laziest Pokémon, but actually it's storing up energy for a counterattack.

Special Moves

Swagger, Punishment, Hammer Arm

EVOLUTION

Slakoth → Vigoroth → Slaking

49
50-99
100-149
150-199
200-249
250-299
300-349
350-399
400-449
450-491

NINCADA

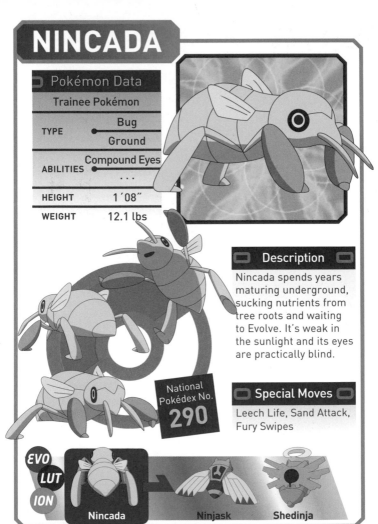

Pokémon Data

Trainee Pokémon

TYPE	Bug
	Ground
ABILITIES	Compound Eyes
	. . .
HEIGHT	1´08˝
WEIGHT	12.1 lbs

Description

Nincada spends years maturing underground, sucking nutrients from tree roots and waiting to Evolve. It's weak in the sunlight and its eyes are practically blind.

Special Moves

Leech Life, Sand Attack, Fury Swipes

National Pokédex No.
290

EVOLUTION

Nincada → Ninjask → Shedinja

NINJASK

1-49
50-99
100-149
150-199
200-249
250-299
300-349
350-399
400-449
450-491

Pokémon Data

Ninja Pokémon

TYPE	Bug
	Flying
ABILITIES	Speed Boost
	. . .
HEIGHT	2′07″
WEIGHT	26.5 lbs

National Pokédex No.
291

Description

Because Ninjask moves so quickly, it's difficult to see its physical form. At one time, it was assumed to be invisible because it was only ever heard, not seen. It loves to eat sweet sap.

Special Moves

Double Team, Slash, Agility

EVO LUT ION

Nincada → Ninjask

SHEDINJA

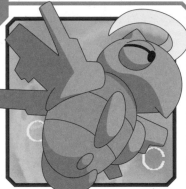

Pokémon Data

Shed Pokémon	
TYPE	Bug
	Ghost
ABILITIES	Wonder Guard
	...
HEIGHT	2´07″
WEIGHT	2.6 lbs

Description

A Pokémon that is actually a soul housed in a cast-off shell. It does not move at all and does not even breathe. It is said that looking into the hole in its back can suck out one's soul.

National Pokédex No.
292

Special Moves

Leech Life, Spite, Grudge, Shadow Sneak

EVO LUT ION

Nincada → Shedinja

WHISMUR

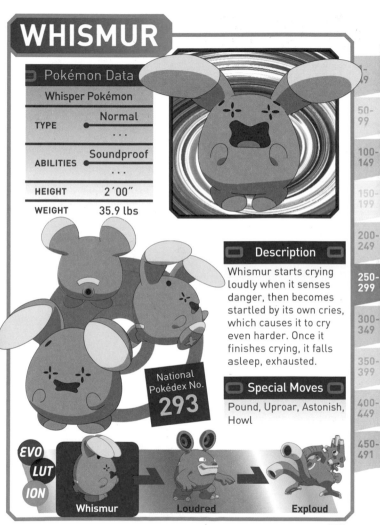

1-
49

50-
99

100-
149

150-
199

200-
249

250-
299

300-
349

350-
399

400-
449

450-
491

Pokémon Data

Whisper Pokémon

TYPE	Normal ...
ABILITIES	Soundproof ...
HEIGHT	2′00″
WEIGHT	35.9 lbs

National Pokédex No.

293

Description

Whismur starts crying loudly when it senses danger, then becomes startled by its own cries, which causes it to cry even harder. Once it finishes crying, it falls asleep, exhausted.

Special Moves

Pound, Uproar, Astonish, Howl

EVO LUT ION

Whismur → Loudred → Exploud

LOUDRED

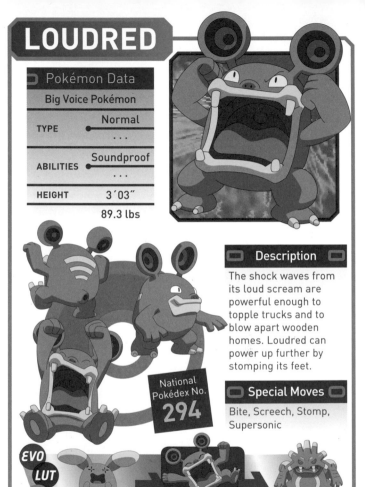

Pokémon Data

Big Voice Pokémon

TYPE	Normal . . .
ABILITIES	Soundproof . . .
HEIGHT	3′03″

89.3 lbs

Description

The shock waves from its loud scream are powerful enough to topple trucks and to blow apart wooden homes. Loudred can power up further by stomping its feet.

Special Moves

Bite, Screech, Stomp, Supersonic

National Pokédex No.
294

EVO LUT ION

Whismur　　Loudred　　Exploud

EXPLOUD

1-49
50-99
100-149
150-199
200-249
250-299
300-349
350-399
400-449
450-491

Pokémon Data

Loud Noise Pokémon

TYPE	Normal . . .
ABILITIES	Soundproof . . .
HEIGHT	4′11″
WEIGHT	185.2 lbs

Description

Exploud emits various sounds from openings all over its body. It uses flute-like sounds to communicate with its friends. Loud roars are reserved for battle.

National Pokédex No.
295

Special Moves

Roar, Stomp, Hyper Beam, Hyper Voice

EVO LUT ION

Whismur → Loudred → Exploud

053

MAKUHITA

Pokémon Data

Guts Pokémon

TYPE	Fighting
	...
ABILITIES	Thick Fat
	Guts
HEIGHT	3′03″
WEIGHT	190.5 lbs

National Pokédex No.
296

Description

Makuhita toughens up its body by ramming against big trees. It trains constantly so that it can become stronger. It will keep getting up no matter how many times it's knocked down.

Special Moves

Arm Thrust, Vital Throw, Whirlwind, Smelling Salts

EVO LUT ION

Makuhita → Hariyama

HARIYAMA

Pokémon Data

Arm Thrust Pokémon

TYPE	Fighting
	...
ABILITIES	Thick Fat
	Guts
HEIGHT	7′07″
WEIGHT	559.5 lbs

National Pokédex No.
297

Description

When Hariyama tenses up its muscles, they become hard as stone, and it can knock aside trucks with a slap of its hand. It likes to test its strength against other large Pokémon.

Special Moves

Force Palm, Seismic Toss, Wake-Up Slap

EVO LUT ION

Makuhita → Hariyama

1-49
50-99
100-149
150-199
200-249
250-299
300-349
350-399
400-449
450-491

AZURILL

Pokémon Data

Polka Dot Pokémon

TYPE	Normal
	. . .
ABILITIES	Thick Fat
	Huge Power
HEIGHT	0´08˝
WEIGHT	4.4 lbs

National Pokédex No.
298

Description

The ball at the end of Azurill's tail is stuffed with nutrients essential to its growth. It fights by whipping opponents with its tail, which is larger than its own body.

Special Moves

Charm, Tail Whip, Slam

EVOLUTION

Azurill → Marill → Azumarill

NOSEPASS

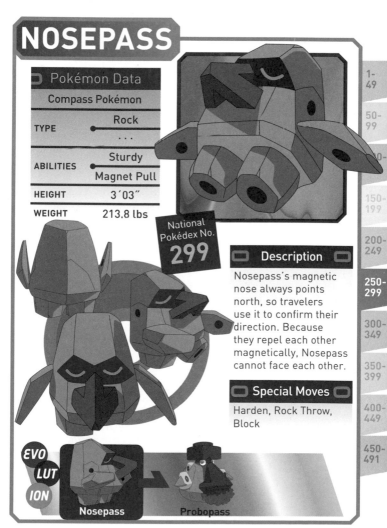

Pokémon Data

Compass Pokémon

TYPE	Rock
	...
ABILITIES	Sturdy
	Magnet Pull
HEIGHT	3´03˝
WEIGHT	213.8 lbs

National Pokédex No.
299

Description

Nosepass's magnetic nose always points north, so travelers use it to confirm their direction. Because they repel each other magnetically, Nosepass cannot face each other.

Special Moves

Harden, Rock Throw, Block

EVOLUTION

Nosepass → Probopass

1-49
50-99
100-
150-199
200-249
250-299
300-349
350-399
400-449
450-491

SKITTY

Pokémon Data

Kitten Pokémon

TYPE	Normal
	. . .
ABILITIES	Cute Charm
	Normalize
HEIGHT	2′00″
WEIGHT	24.3 lbs

Description

Skitty lives in trees and has a habit of chasing anything that moves. Sometimes it spins in place while chasing its own tail.

National Pokédex No.

300

Special Moves

Copycat, Assist, Charm, Captivate

EVO LUT ION

Skitty → Delcatty

DELCATTY

Pokémon Data

Prim Pokémon

TYPE	Normal
	...
ABILITIES	Cute Charm
	Normalize
HEIGHT	3′07″
WEIGHT	71.09 lbs

National Pokédex No.
301

1-49
50-99
100-149
150-199
200-249
250-299
300-349
350-399
400-449
450-491

Description

Delcatty is a popular Pokémon thanks to its beautiful fur. It does not keep a nest, and if another Pokémon approaches, it will yield without a fight and find another place to sleep.

Special Moves

Fake Out, Attract, Double Slap

EVOLUTION

Skitty → Delcatty

SABLEYE

Pokémon Data

Darkness Pokémon

TYPE	Dark
	Ghost
ABILITIES	Keen Eye
	Stall
HEIGHT	1'08"
WEIGHT	24.3 lbs

National Pokédex No.
302

Description

Sableye lives inside caves and loves to eat gems so much that its eyes have turned into gems themselves. You can see its eyes glitter in the darkness.

Special Moves

Shadow Sneak, Shadow Claw, Confuse Ray, Power Gem

EVO LUT ION

Sableye

Does not Evolve

MAWILE

Pokémon Data

Deceiver Pokémon

TYPE	Steel ...
ABILITIES	Hyper-Cutter Intimidate
HEIGHT	2'00"
WEIGHT	25.4 lbs

National Pokédex No.
303

Description

The gigantic jaw on its head has enough power to cut through steel. If an opponent lets its guard down because of Mawile's cute and innocent face, it will get bitten.

Special Moves

Astonish, Vice Grip, Crunch, Fake Tears

EVO LUT ION

Mawile — Does not Evolve

1-49
50-99
100-149
150-199
200-249
250-299
300-349
350-399
400-449
450-491

ARON

Pokémon Data

Iron Armor Pokémon

TYPE	Steel
	Rock
ABILITIES	Sturdy
	Rock Head
HEIGHT	1´04˝
WEIGHT	132.3 lbs

National Pokédex No.
304

Description

Aron lives deep within mountains and survives by eating iron ore. On the rare occasion that it leaves the mountains, it eats train tracks, cars, or anything else with a lot of iron.

Special Moves

Iron Defense, Take Down, Headbutt, Metal Claw

EVOLUTION

Aron

Lairon

Aggron

LAIRON

1–49
50–99
100–149
150–199
200–249
250–299
300–349
350–399
400–449
450–491

Pokémon Data

Iron Armor Pokémon	
TYPE	Steel
	Rock
ABILITIES	Sturdy
	Rock Head
HEIGHT	2´11˝
WEIGHT	264.6 lbs

National Pokédex No.
305

Description

Lairon creates nests next to springs and engages in territorial fights. Since it eats iron, it sometimes also gets into fights with humans who come to mine iron ore near its nests.

Special Moves

Iron Head, Protect, Metal Sound

EVO LUT ION

Aron

Lairon

Aggron

063

AGGRON

Pokémon Data

Iron Armor Pokémon

TYPE	Steel
	Rock
ABILITIES	Sturdy
	Rock Head
HEIGHT	6´11″
WEIGHT	793.7 lbs

National Pokédex No.
306

Description

Aggron digs tunnels through mountains in search of iron. After a mountain's ore is depleted, Aggron moves earth, replants trees and cleans up.

Special Moves

Iron Tail, Double-Edge, Metal Burst

EVO LUT ION

Aron → Lairon → Aggron

MEDITITE

Pokémon Data

Meditate Pokémon

TYPE	Fighting
	Psychic
ABILITIES	Pure Power
	...
HEIGHT	2'00"
WEIGHT	24.7 lbs

National Pokédex No.
307

Description

It trains in yoga every day, increasing the strength of its willpower through meditation. However, because Meditite has a short attention span, it never finishes its training.

Special Moves

Meditate, Confusion, Mind Reader

EVO LUT ION

Meditite → Medicham

1-49
50-99
100-149
150-199
200-249
250-299
300-349
350-399
400-449
450-491

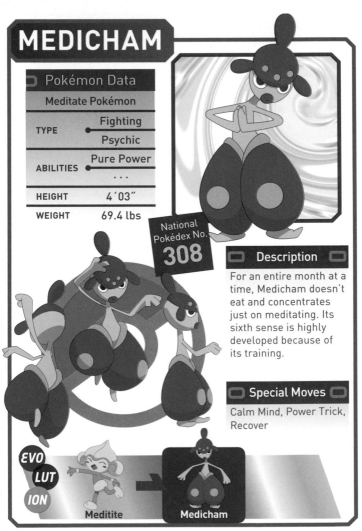

MEDICHAM

Pokémon Data

Meditate Pokémon	
TYPE	Fighting
	Psychic
ABILITIES	Pure Power
	...
HEIGHT	4´03˝
WEIGHT	69.4 lbs

National
Pokédex No.
308

Description

For an entire month at a time, Medicham doesn't eat and concentrates just on meditating. Its sixth sense is highly developed because of its training.

Special Moves

Calm Mind, Power Trick, Recover

EVOLUTION

Meditite → Medicham

ELECTRIKE

Pokémon Data

Lightning Pokémon

TYPE	Electric
	...
ABILITIES	Static
	Lightning Rod
HEIGHT	2'00"
WEIGHT	33.5 lbs

National Pokédex No.
309

Description

Electrike stores the electric charge that's created by the friction of air molecules against its long fur when it's running. It uses the stored power to run.

Special Moves

Thunder Wave, Howl, Spark, Quick Attack

EVO LUT ION

Electrike → Manectric

1-49

100-149

150-199

200-249

250-299

300-349

350-399

400-449

450-491

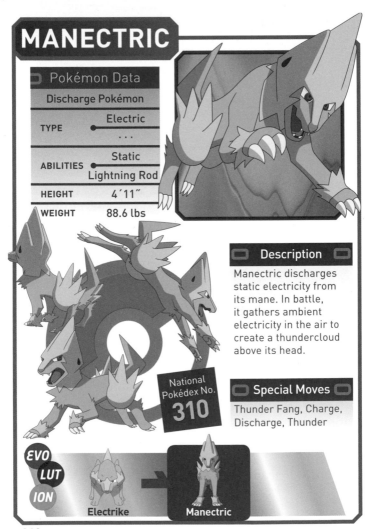

MANECTRIC

Pokémon Data

Discharge Pokémon

TYPE	Electric
	. . .
ABILITIES	Static
	Lightning Rod
HEIGHT	4´11˝
WEIGHT	88.6 lbs

Description

Manectric discharges static electricity from its mane. In battle, it gathers ambient electricity in the air to create a thundercloud above its head.

National Pokédex No. **310**

Special Moves

Thunder Fang, Charge, Discharge, Thunder

EVOLUTION

Electrike → Manectric

PLUSLE

Pokémon Data

Cheering Pokémon

TYPE	Electric . . .
ABILITIES	Plus . . .
HEIGHT	1´04˝
WEIGHT	9.3 lbs

1-
49

50-
99

100-
149

150-
199

200-
249

250-
299

300-
349

350-
399

400-
449

450-
491

Description

Plusle cheers its friends on with pompoms made of fire sparks. When it's cheering, its body glows with fire sparks. If its friends lose, it will cry loudly.

Special Moves

Helping Hand, Encore, Thunder, Swift

National Pokédex No.
311

EVO LUT ION

Plusle — Does not Evolve

MINUN

Pokémon Data

Cheering Pokémon

TYPE	Electric . . .
ABILITIES	Minus . . .
HEIGHT	1´04˝
WEIGHT	9.3 lbs

Description

Minun cheers its friends on with fireworks made from the electricity in its body. When they're in danger of losing, the fireworks get bigger.

National Pokédex No.
312

Special Moves

Helping Hand, Thunder Wave, Trump Card

EVO LUT ION

Minun

Does not Evolve

VOLBEAT

Pokémon Data

Firefly Pokémon

TYPE	Bug
	...
ABILITIES	Illuminate
	Swarm
HEIGHT	2´04˝
WEIGHT	39.0 lbs

1-49

50-99

100-149

150-199

200-249

250-299

300-349

350-399

400-449

450-491

Description

When night falls, it communicates with its friends by blinking the light on its rear. Lured by Illumise's Sweet Scent, Volbeat gather together and draw light patterns in the night sky.

Special Moves

Tail Glow, Protect, Zen Headbutt

National Pokédex No.

313

EVO *LUT* *ION*

Volbeat

Does not Evolve

071

ILLUMISE

Pokémon Data

Firefly Pokémon

TYPE	Bug
	...
ABILITIES	Oblivious
	Tinted Lens
HEIGHT	2´00˝
WEIGHT	39.0 lbs

Description

Illumise attracts Volbeat with Sweet Scent, then performs a dance drawing geometric designs in the night sky. The more complicated the designs, the greater the respect it earns from its group.

National Pokédex No.
314

Special Moves

Wish, Flatter, Bug Buzz

EVO LUT ION

Illumise

Does not Evolve

ROSELIA

Pokémon Data

Thorn Pokémon

TYPE	Grass
	Poison
ABILITIES	Natural Cure
	Poison Point
HEIGHT	1´00″
WEIGHT	4.4 lbs

Description

Poisonous thorns are hidden in Roselia's flower hands. It fires these thorns at anyone who goes after its flowers. The scent of the flowers creates a relaxed feeling.

Special Moves

Sweet Scent, Toxic, Petal Dance

National Pokédex No.
315

1–49

50–99

100–149

150–199

200–249

250–299

300–349

350–399

400–449

450–491

EVO LUT ION

Budew

Roselia

Roserade

GULPIN

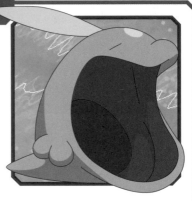

Pokémon Data

Stomach Pokémon

TYPE	Poison
	. . .
ABILITIES	Liquid Ooze
	Sticky Hold
HEIGHT	1′04″
WEIGHT	22.7 lbs

Description

Gulpin's body is almost all stomach. Its heart and brain are very small. It can swallow whole anything up to its own size.

National Pokédex No.

316

Special Moves

Poison Gas, Sludge, Amnesia, Yawn

EVO LUT ION

Gulpin → Swalot

SWALOT

1-49
50-99
100-149
150-199
200-249
250-299
300-349
350-399
400-449
450-491

Pokémon Data

Poison Bag Pokémon

TYPE	Poison
	. . .
ABILITIES	Liquid Ooze
	Sticky Hold
HEIGHT	5´07˝
WEIGHT	176.4 lbs

National Pokédex No. **317**

Description

Because Swalot has no teeth, it swallows anything and everything whole. It sprays deadly poison from its follicles to capture its prey. Once the prey is weakened, it swallows it up.

Special Moves

Toxic, Gastro Acid, Gunk Shot

EVO LUT ION

Gulpin → Swalot

CARVANHA

Pokémon Data

Savage Pokémon

TYPE	Water
	Dark
ABILITIES	Rough Skin
	. . .
HEIGHT	2´07˝
WEIGHT	45.9 lbs

National Pokédex No.
318

Description

With their sharp fangs and overdeveloped lower jaws, Carvanha can even chomp through boats. When an enemy enters Carvanha territory, they attack as a group.

Special Moves

Rage, Ice Fang, Swagger, Crunch

EVO LUT ION

Carvanha → Sharpedo

SHARPEDO

Pokémon Data

Brutal Pokémon

TYPE	Water
	Dark
ABILITIES	Rough Skin
	. . .
HEIGHT	5′11″
WEIGHT	195.8 lbs

National Pokédex No. **319**

Description

Sharpedo can swim as fast as 75 mph. However, it cannot travel long distances. Its teeth, which are hard enough to chew up steel plates, quickly grow back if they're broken off.

Special Moves

Aqua Jet, Skull Bash, Night Slash

 EVO LUT ION

 Carvanha → Sharpedo

1-49
50-99
100-149
150-199
200-249
250-299
300-349
350-399
400-449
450-491

WAILMER

Pokémon Data

Ball Whale Pokémon

TYPE	Water · · ·
ABILITIES	Water Veil / Oblivious
HEIGHT	6´07˝
WEIGHT	286.6 lbs

National Pokédex No.
320

Description

Wailmer plays by filling its body with water and bouncing around on the beach. The more water it takes in, the higher it can jump. It sprays seawater out from the nostrils above its eyes.

Special Moves

Water Gun, Whirlpool, Water Pulse

EVO LUT ION

Wailmer

Wailord

WAILORD

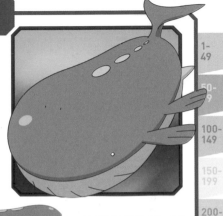

Pokémon Data

Float Whale Pokémon

TYPE	Water
	...
ABILITIES	Water Veil
	Oblivious
HEIGHT	47´07˝
WEIGHT	877.4 lbs

National Pokédex No.
321

Description

Wailord is the largest Pokémon. It can dive down to a depth of almost 10,000 feet without taking a breath.

Special Moves

Water Spout, Dive, Hydro Pump

1-
49

50-
9

100-
149

150-
199

200-
249

250-
299

300-
349

350-
399

400-
449

450-
491

EVO
LUT
ION

Wailmer   Wailord

NUMEL

Pokémon Data

Numb Pokémon

TYPE	Fire
	Ground
ABILITIES	Oblivious
	Simple
HEIGHT	2′04″
WEIGHT	52.9 lbs

National Pokédex No.
322

Description

In its hump it stores magma that is at a temperature of over 1,200°F. When it rains, the magma cools and Numel's movements slow.

Special Moves

Magnitude, Take Down, Lava Plume

EVO LUT ION

Numel → Camerupt

CAMERUPT

1-49
50-99
100-149
150-199
200-249
250-299
300-349
350-399
400-449
450-491

Pokémon Data

Eruption Pokémon

TYPE	Fire
	Ground
ABILITIES	Magma Armor
	Solid Rock
HEIGHT	6'03"
WEIGHT	485.0 lbs

National Pokédex No.
323

Description

On its back are volcano-shaped humps that are actually bones. The magma in the humps is kept at a temperature of almost 10,000°F.

Special Moves

Earth Power, Earthquake, Eruption, Fissure

EVO LUT ION

Numel → Camerupt

TORKOAL

Pokémon Data

Coal Pokémon

TYPE	Fire
	. . .
ABILITIES	White Smoke
	. . .
HEIGHT	1´08˝
WEIGHT	177.2 lbs

National Pokédex No.

324

Description

Torkoal burns coal inside its shell and converts it into energy. When it finds itself in a pinch, it blows out a cloud of black smoke as cover for escape.

Special Moves

Withdraw, Rapid Spin, Lava Plume

EVOLUTION

Torkoal

Does not Evolve

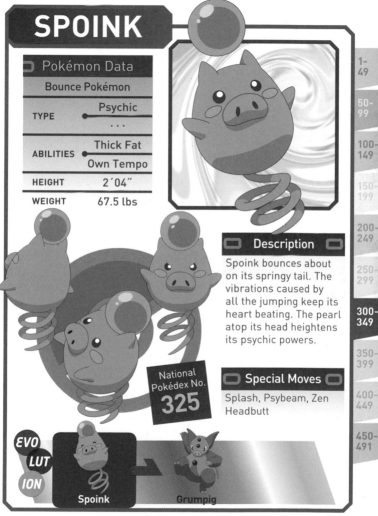

SPOINK

Pokémon Data

Bounce Pokémon

TYPE	Psychic ...
ABILITIES	Thick Fat Own Tempo
HEIGHT	2´04˝
WEIGHT	67.5 lbs

Description

Spoink bounces about on its springy tail. The vibrations caused by all the jumping keep its heart beating. The pearl atop its head heightens its psychic powers.

National Pokédex No.
325

Special Moves

Splash, Psybeam, Zen Headbutt

EVO LUT ION

Spoink → Grumpig

1–49
50–99
100–149
150–199
200–249
250–299
300–349
350–399
400–449
450–491

GRUMPIG

Pokémon Data

Manipulate Pokémon

TYPE	Psychic
	...
ABILITIES	Thick Fat
	Own Tempo
HEIGHT	2´11"
WEIGHT	157.6 lbs

National Pokédex No.
326

Description

Grumpig can manipulate its opponents using a mysterious dance. Its psychic powers are amplified through the black pearls on its body.

Special Moves

Payback, Power Gem, Psychic

EVOLUTION

Spoink → Grumpig

SPINDA

Pokémon Data

Spot Panda Pokémon

TYPE	Normal
	...
ABILITIES	Own Tempo
	Tangled Feet
HEIGHT	3´07"
WEIGHT	11.0 lbs

National
Pokédex No.
327

Description

Every Spinda has a different pattern of spots: no two are exactly the same. The pattern confuses opponents, and Spinda throws off their aim even more with its unsteady movements.

Special Moves

Teeter Dance, Flail, Dizzy Punch

EVO
LUT
ION

Spinda

Does not Evolve

1-49
50-99
100-149
150-199
200-249
250-299
300-349
350-399
400-449
450-491

TRAPINCH

Pokémon Data

Ant Pit Pokémon

TYPE	Ground . . .
ABILITIES	Hyper Cutter Arena Trap
HEIGHT	2´04″
WEIGHT	33.1 lbs

National Pokédex No.

328

Description

Trapinch digs a hole in the desert sand and waits for prey to fall in. Once the prey falls in the hole, it cannot escape. Trapinch can survive for a week without water.

Special Moves

Sand Tomb, Crunch, Dig

EVO LUT ION

Trapinch → Vibrava → Flygon

VIBRAVA

Pokémon Data

Vibration Pokémon

| TYPE | Ground |
| | Dragon |

| ABILITIES | Levitate |
| | . . . |

| HEIGHT | 3´07˝ |
| WEIGHT | 33.7 lbs |

National Pokédex No.
329

1–
49

50–
99

100–
149

150–
199

200–
249

250–
299

300–
349

350–
399

400–
449

450–
491

Description

Vibrava creates powerful ultrasonic waves by rapidly flapping its double wings. Since its wings are still growing, it's better at creating these waves than it is at flying.

Special Moves

Supersonic, Sonic Boom, Screech

EVO LUT ION

Trapinch   Vibrava   Flygon

FLYGON

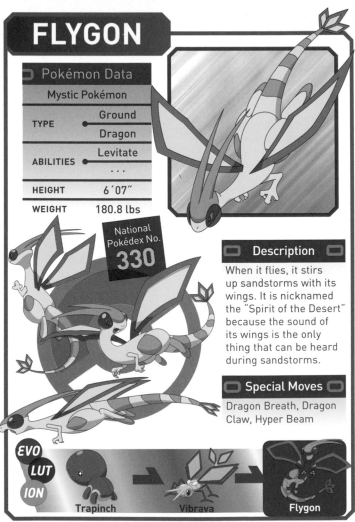

Pokémon Data

Mystic Pokémon

TYPE	Ground
	Dragon
ABILITIES	Levitate
	...
HEIGHT	6´07"
WEIGHT	180.8 lbs

National Pokédex No.
330

Description

When it flies, it stirs up sandstorms with its wings. It is nicknamed the "Spirit of the Desert" because the sound of its wings is the only thing that can be heard during sandstorms.

Special Moves

Dragon Breath, Dragon Claw, Hyper Beam

EVO LUT ION

Trapinch → Vibrava → Flygon

CACNEA

Pokémon Data

Cactus Pokémon

TYPE	Grass
	...
ABILITIES	Sand Veil
	...
HEIGHT	1´04"
WEIGHT	113.1 lbs

National Pokédex No.
331

Description

Cacnea lives in very dry areas. It stores water in its body and can survive without drinking for at least thirty days. It fights using its spike-covered arms.

Special Moves

Growth, Leech Seed, Pin Missile

EVOLUTION

Cacnea → Cacturne

1–49
50–99
100–149
150–199
200–249
250–299
300–349
350–399
400–449
450–491

CACTURNE

Pokémon Data

Scarecrow Pokémon

TYPE	Grass
	Dark

ABILITIES	Sand Veil
	...

HEIGHT	4´03″
WEIGHT	170.6 lbs

Description

Cacturne stays very still during the day. When night falls and the temperature cools, it becomes active. It looks for prey that has succumbed to the desert's heat.

National Pokédex No.
332

Special Moves

Feint Attack, Sucker Punch, Needle Arm

 EVO LUT ION

 Cacnea → Cacturne

090

SWABLU

Pokémon Data

Cotton Bird Pokémon

TYPE	Normal
	Flying
ABILITIES	Natural Cure
	. . .
HEIGHT	1´04"
WEIGHT	2.6 lbs

Description

Swablu has fluffy, cottony wings that look like clouds. When its wings become dirty, it heads to the river to play in the water.

Special Moves

Sing, Fury Attack, Natural Gift

National Pokédex No.

333

EVOLUTION

Swablu → Altaria

1-49
50-99
100-149
150-199
200-249
250-299
300-349
350-399
400-449
450-491

ALTARIA

Pokémon Data

Humming Pokémon

TYPE	Dragon
	Flying
ABILITIES	Natural Cure
	. . .
HEIGHT	3′07″
WEIGHT	45.4 lbs

National Pokédex No.
334

Description

Altaria floats on wings like puffy clouds, riding the air currents. It sings with a very high, pure voice. Those who hear its song become entranced by it.

Special Moves

Refresh, Dragon Dance, Perish Song

EVOLUTION

Swablu → Altaria

ZANGOOSE

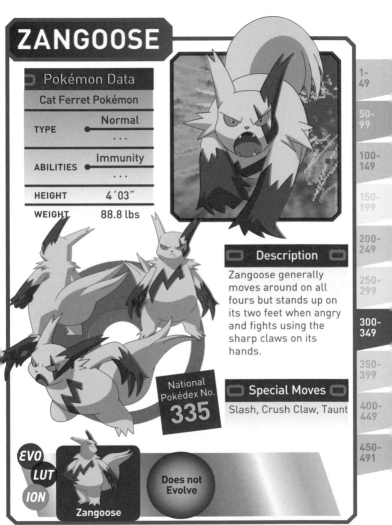

Pokémon Data

Cat Ferret Pokémon

TYPE
Normal
. . .

ABILITIES
Immunity
. . .

HEIGHT 4´03˝

WEIGHT 88.8 lbs

Description

Zangoose generally moves around on all fours but stands up on its two feet when angry and fights using the sharp claws on its hands.

National Pokédex No.
335

Special Moves

Slash, Crush Claw, Taunt

EVO
LUT
ION

Zangoose

Does not Evolve

1-49

50-99

100-149

150-199

200-249

250-299

300-349

350-399

400-449

450-491

SEVIPER

Pokémon Data

Fang Snake Pokémon

TYPE	Poison ...
ABILITIES	Shed Skin ...
HEIGHT	8´10˝
WEIGHT	115.7 lbs

National Pokédex No.
336

Description

Seviper prepares for battle by sharpening its tail blade on boulders. An opponent slashed by this blade quickly succumbs to the poison on it.

Special Moves

Poison Jab, Poison Fang, Poison Tail, Glare

EVO LUT ION

Seviper

Does not Evolve

LUNATONE

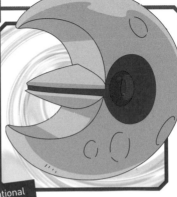

Pokémon Data

Meteorite Pokémon

TYPE	Rock
	Psychic
ABILITIES	Levitate
	...
HEIGHT	3´03˝
WEIGHT	370.4 lbs

National Pokédex No.
337

1-49
50-99
100-149
150-199
200-249
250-299
300-349
350-399
400-449
450-491

Description

Lunatone was found at the location where a meteorite fell to earth. It becomes very active on full-moon nights. Looking directly into its red eyes can cause paralysis.

Special Moves

Rock Throw, Cosmic Power, Psychic

EVOLUTION

Lunatone → Does not Evolve

SOLROCK

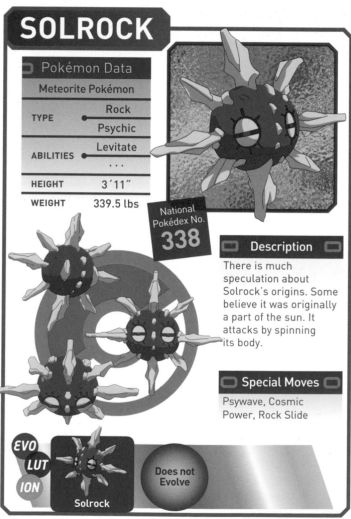

Pokémon Data

Meteorite Pokémon

TYPE	Rock
	Psychic
ABILITIES	Levitate
	. . .
HEIGHT	3´11″
WEIGHT	339.5 lbs

National Pokédex No.
338

Description

There is much speculation about Solrock's origins. Some believe it was originally a part of the sun. It attacks by spinning its body.

Special Moves

Psywave, Cosmic Power, Rock Slide

EVO LUT ION

Solrock

Does not Evolve

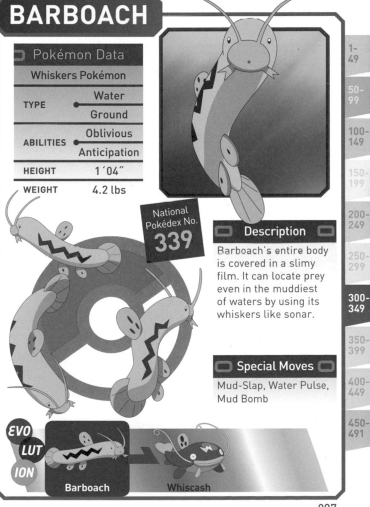

BARBOACH

Pokémon Data

Whiskers Pokémon

TYPE	Water
	Ground
ABILITIES	Oblivious
	Anticipation
HEIGHT	1'04"
WEIGHT	4.2 lbs

National Pokédex No.
339

1–49
50–99
100–149
150–199
200–249
250–299
300–349
350–399
400–449
450–491

Description

Barboach's entire body is covered in a slimy film. It can locate prey even in the muddiest of waters by using its whiskers like sonar.

Special Moves

Mud-Slap, Water Pulse, Mud Bomb

EVO LUT ION

Barboach → Whiscash

WHISCASH

Pokémon Data

Whiskers Pokémon

TYPE	Water
	Ground
ABILITIES	Oblivious
	Anticipation
HEIGHT	2´11˝
WEIGHT	52.0 lbs

National Pokédex No.

340

Description

Whiscash is strongly protective of its territory. If an enemy approaches, it will use Earthquake. It also has the power to foresee natural earthquakes.

Special Moves

Water Pulse, Fissure, Earthquake, Aqua Tail

EVO LUT ION

Barboach → Whiscash

CORPHISH

Pokémon Data

Ruffian Pokémon

TYPE	Water . . .
ABILITIES	Hyper Cutter Shell Armor
HEIGHT	2′00″
WEIGHT	25.4 lbs

Description

Corphish's sharp claws help it keep a strong hold on its prey. It is very hardy and can live pretty much anywhere. Originally it was a pet Pokémon imported from abroad.

Special Moves

Vice Grip, Bubble Beam, Protect, Knock Off

National Pokédex No.
341

EVO LUT ION

Corphish

Crawdaunt

60-99
100-149
150-199
200-249
250-299
300-349
350-399
400-449
450-491

CRAWDAUNT

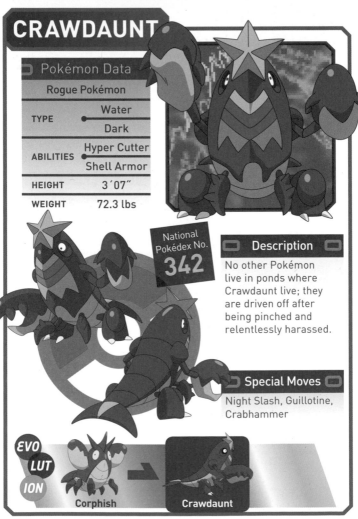

Pokémon Data

Rogue Pokémon

TYPE	Water
	Dark
ABILITIES	Hyper Cutter
	Shell Armor
HEIGHT	3´07"
WEIGHT	72.3 lbs

National Pokédex No.
342

Description

No other Pokémon live in ponds where Crawdaunt live; they are driven off after being pinched and relentlessly harassed.

Special Moves

Night Slash, Guillotine, Crabhammer

EVOLUTION

Corphish → Crawdaunt

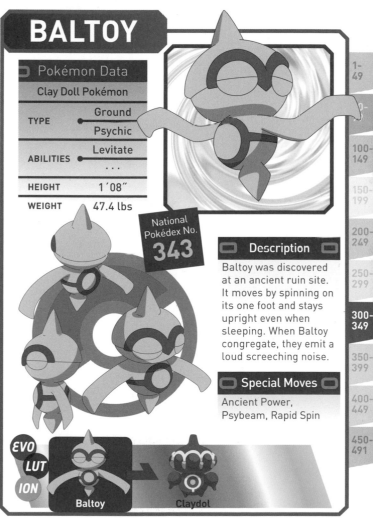

BALTOY

Pokémon Data

Clay Doll Pokémon

TYPE	Ground
	Psychic
ABILITIES	Levitate
	. . .
HEIGHT	1´08˝
WEIGHT	47.4 lbs

National Pokédex No.

343

Description

Baltoy was discovered at an ancient ruin site. It moves by spinning on its one foot and stays upright even when sleeping. When Baltoy congregate, they emit a loud screeching noise.

Special Moves

Ancient Power, Psybeam, Rapid Spin

EVO LUT ION

Baltoy → Claydol

1-49
100-149
150-199
200-249
250-299
300-349
350-399
400-449
450-491

CLAYDOL

Pokémon Data

Clay Doll Pokémon

TYPE	Ground
	Psychic
ABILITIES	Levitate
	...
HEIGHT	4´11˝
WEIGHT	238.1 lbs

National Pokédex No.
344

Description

A 20,000-year-old mud doll made by an ancient civilization, Claydol became a Pokémon after being exposed to mysterious energy rays. It can shoot light beams from both arms.

Special Moves

Hyper Beam, Explosion, Ancient Power, Cosmic Power

EVO LUT ION

Baltoy → Claydol

102

LILEEP

1-
49

50-
99

100-
149

150-
199

200-
249

250-
299

300-
349

350-
399

400-
449

450-
491

Pokémon Data

Sea Lily Pokémon

| TYPE | Rock |
| | Grass |

| ABILITIES | Suction Cups |
| | . . . |

| HEIGHT | 3´03˝ |
| WEIGHT | 52.5 lbs |

National
Pokédex No.
345

Description

An ancient Pokémon
resurrected from a
fossil, Lileep can be
found clinging to rocks
on the sea bottom.
It uses its petal-like
tentacles to snag prey
that wanders too close.

Special Moves

Ingrain, Acid, Confuse
Ray

**EVO
LUT
ION**

Lileep   Cradily

103

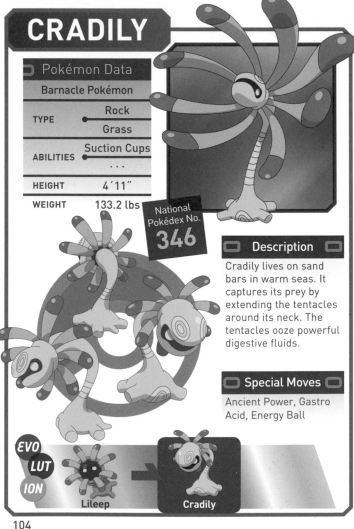

CRADILY

Pokémon Data

Barnacle Pokémon

TYPE	Rock
	Grass
ABILITIES	Suction Cups
	...
HEIGHT	4′11″
WEIGHT	133.2 lbs

National Pokédex No.

346

Description

Cradily lives on sand bars in warm seas. It captures its prey by extending the tentacles around its neck. The tentacles ooze powerful digestive fluids.

Special Moves

Ancient Power, Gastro Acid, Energy Ball

EVOLUTION

Lileep → Cradily

ANORITH

Pokémon Data

Old Shrimp Pokémon

TYPE	Rock
	Bug
ABILITIES	Battle Armor
	. . .
HEIGHT	2´04˝
WEIGHT	27.6 lbs

National Pokédex No.
347

Description

A Pokémon resurrected by scientists from an ancient fossil. It grabs its prey by using its two extending claws and swims by wriggling its eight swimmerets.

Special Moves

Protect, Ancient Power, Fury Cutter

EVOLUTION

Anorith → Armaldo

1-49
50-99
100-149
150-199
200-249
250-299
300-349
350-399
400-449
450-491

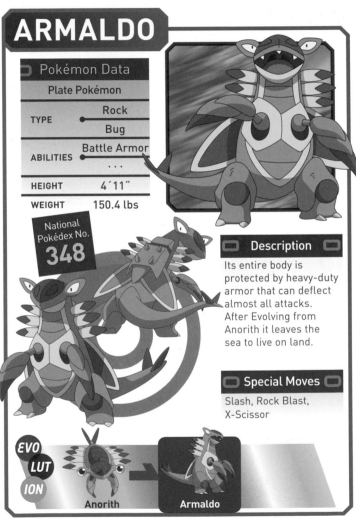

ARMALDO

Pokémon Data

Plate Pokémon

TYPE	Rock
	Bug
ABILITIES	Battle Armor
	...
HEIGHT	4′11″
WEIGHT	150.4 lbs

National Pokédex No.
348

Description

Its entire body is protected by heavy-duty armor that can deflect almost all attacks. After Evolving from Anorith it leaves the sea to live on land.

Special Moves

Slash, Rock Blast, X-Scissor

EVOLUTION

Anorith → Armaldo

106

FEEBAS

Pokémon Data

Fish Pokémon

TYPE	Water . . .
ABILITIES	Swift Swim . . .
HEIGHT	2´00˝
WEIGHT	16.3 lbs

National Pokédex No.
349

Description

Because it is so homely, Feebas never attracts any attention. Since it can eat pretty much anything, it can survive in polluted rivers and lakes.

Special Moves

Splash, Tackle, Flail

EVOLUTION

Feebas → Milotic

1-49
50-99
100-149
150-199
200-249
250-299
300-349
350-399
400-449
450-491

MILOTIC

Pokémon Data

Tender Pokémon

TYPE	Water
	...
ABILITIES	Marvel Scale
	...
HEIGHT	20´04˝
WEIGHT	357.1 lbs

National Pokédex No.
350

Description

One of the most beautiful Pokémon, Milotic lives in deep lakes. When conflict rages, it emerges from the lake and emits a healing energy to calm people's hearts.

Special Moves

Hydro Pump, Aqua Ring, Captivate, Aqua Tail

EVO LUT ION

Feebas → Milotic

CASTFORM

1-49
50-99
100-149
150-199
200-249
250-299
300-349
350-399
400-449
450-491

Pokémon Data

Weather Pokémon

TYPE	Normal ···
ABILITIES	Forecast ···
HEIGHT	1'00"
WEIGHT	1.8 lbs

National Pokédex No.
351

Snow Form

Sun Form

Rain Form

Description

In order to protect itself, Castform uses the power of nature, changing its appearance with the weather.

Special Moves

Weather Ball, Rain Dance, Sunny Day, Hail

EVOLUTION

Castform → Does not Evolve

KECLEON

Pokémon Data

Color Swap Pokémon

TYPE	Normal
	. . .
ABILITIES	Color Change
	. . .
HEIGHT	3´03˝
WEIGHT	48.5 lbs

National Pokédex No.
352

Description

Kecleon can change its body color and gets close to its prey by blending in with its surroundings. However, it can't camouflage the zigzag pattern around its belly.

Special Moves

Lick, Feint Attack, Fury Swipes

EVOLUTION

Kecleon

Does not Evolve

SHUPPET

Pokémon Data

Puppet Pokémon

TYPE	Ghost
	. . .
ABILITIES	Insomnia
	Frisk
HEIGHT	2′00″
WEIGHT	5.1 lbs

National Pokédex No.
353

Description

It loves the human emotions of spite and envy. Shuppet can be found hanging under the eaves of the houses of those who harbor great malice or envy.

Special Moves

Night Shade, Curse, Spite, Shadow Sneak

EVO LUT ION

Shuppet → Banette

1–49
50–99
100–149
150–199
200–249
250–299
300–349
350–399
400–449
450–491

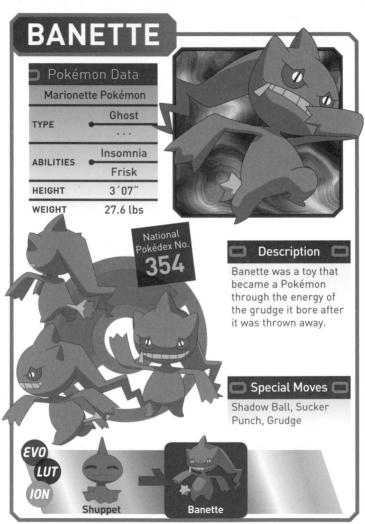

BANETTE

Pokémon Data

Marionette Pokémon

TYPE	Ghost
	...
ABILITIES	Insomnia
	Frisk
HEIGHT	3'07"
WEIGHT	27.6 lbs

National Pokédex No.
354

Description

Banette was a toy that became a Pokémon through the energy of the grudge it bore after it was thrown away.

Special Moves

Shadow Ball, Sucker Punch, Grudge

EVO LUT ION

Shuppet → Banette

DUSKULL

Pokémon Data

Requiem Pokémon

TYPE	Ghost
	. . .
ABILITIES	Levitate
	. . .
HEIGHT	2´07˝
WEIGHT	33.1 lbs

1-49

50-99

100-149

150-199

200-249

250-299

300-349

350-399

400-449

450-491

Description

Duskull wanders about in the darkness in the middle of the night. It's able to slip through even the thickest of walls and will not stop pursuing its prey until the morning light.

Special Moves

Disable, Astonish, Pursuit

National Pokédex No.
355

EVOLUTION

Duskull → Dusclops → Dusknoir

DUSCLOPS

Pokémon Data

Beckon Pokémon

TYPE	Ghost
	...
ABILITIES	Pressure
	...
HEIGHT	5´03˝
WEIGHT	67.5 lbs

National Pokédex No.
356

Description

Dusclops hypnotizes and controls its opponents with the mysterious movements of its hands and single eye. Its body is hollow, and anyone who gazes into it will be sucked into the void.

Special Moves

Shadow Sneak, Curse, Will-O-Wisp, Shadow Punch

EVOLUTION

Duskull → Dusclops → Dusknoir

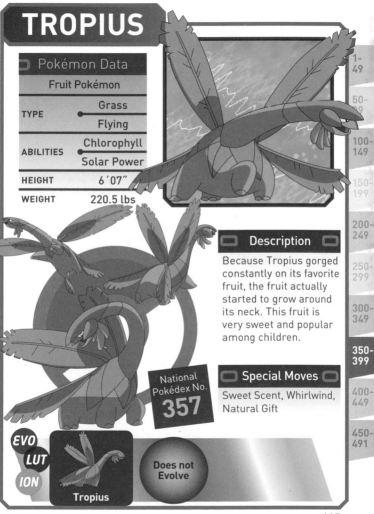

TROPIUS

Pokémon Data

Fruit Pokémon	
TYPE	Grass
	Flying
ABILITIES	Chlorophyll
	Solar Power
HEIGHT	6′07″
WEIGHT	220.5 lbs

Description

Because Tropius gorged constantly on its favorite fruit, the fruit actually started to grow around its neck. This fruit is very sweet and popular among children.

National Pokédex No.
357

Special Moves

Sweet Scent, Whirlwind, Natural Gift

EVOLUTION

Tropius — Does not Evolve

1-49
50-99
100-149
150-199
200-249
250-299
300-349
350-399
400-449
450-491

CHIMECHO

Pokémon Data

Wind Chime Pokémon

TYPE	Psychic . . .
ABILITIES	Levitate . . .
HEIGHT	2´00˝
WEIGHT	2.2 lbs

Description

Chimecho travels long distances by floating along on the wind. It communicates with others of its kind via high-frequency sound waves. When angered, it rings loudly.

Special Moves

Yawn, Heal Bell, Extrasensory

National Pokédex No.

358

EVO LUT ION

Chingling → Chimecho

ABSOL

Pokémon Data

Disaster Pokémon

TYPE	Dark
	...
ABILITIES	Pressure
	Super Luck
HEIGHT	3´11″
WEIGHT	103.6 lbs

1-49

50-99

100-149

150-199

200-249

250-299

300-349

350-399

400-449

450-491

Description

Absol lives alone in the mountains, but whenever it senses an impending catastrophe, it will go and warn humans of the danger. That's why it's called the "Disaster Pokémon."

Special Moves

Razor Wind, Bite, Future Sight, Sucker Punch

National Pokédex No. **359**

EVO LUT ION

Absol — Does not Evolve

117

WYNAUT

Pokémon Data

Bright Pokémon

TYPE	Psychic
	. . .
ABILITIES	Shadow Tag
	. . .
HEIGHT	2´00˝
WEIGHT	30.9 lbs

Description

On moonlit nights, Wynaut train by having shoving matches with each other. You can tell when they're angry because they start thumping the ground with their tails.

National Pokédex No.

360

Special Moves

Mirror Coat, Safeguard, Destiny Bond

EVO LUT ION

Wynaut

Wobbuffet

SNORUNT

Pokémon Data

Snow Hat Pokémon

TYPE	Ice
	...
ABILITIES	Inner Focus
	Ice Body
HEIGHT	2´04˝
WEIGHT	37.0 lbs

National Pokédex No.
361

Description

Snorunt live in places that get lots of snow. During seasons without snow, they live quietly deep inside caves. It is said that any household that has a Snorunt in it becomes prosperous.

Special Moves

Icy Wind, Headbutt, Ice Shard

EVO LUT ION

Snorunt

Glalie

Froslass

1-49
50-99
100-149
150-199
200-249
250-299
300-349
350-399
400-449
450-491

GLALIE

Pokémon Data

Face Pokémon	
TYPE	Ice
	. . .
ABILITIES	Inner Focus
	Ice Body
HEIGHT	4´11˝
WEIGHT	565.5 lbs

Description

Glalie protects itself by encasing its body in an armor of ice that cannot be melted, even with fire. It has the power to generate ice by freezing the moisture in the air.

Special Moves

Ice Fang, Hail, Blizzard, Sheer Cold

National Pokédex No.
362

EVO LUT ION

Snorunt

Glalie

SPHEAL

Pokémon Data

Clap Pokémon

TYPE	Ice
	Water
ABILITIES	Thick Fat
	Ice Body
HEIGHT	2′07″
WEIGHT	87.1 lbs

National Pokédex No.
363

Description

It's easier and faster for Spheal to move by rolling than by walking. Its body shape is ill-suited for swimming as well.

Special Moves

Defense Curl, Ice Ball, Body Slam

EVOLUTION

Spheal → Sealeo → Walrein

1–49
50–99
100–149
150–199
200–249
250–299
300–349
350–399
400–449
450–491

SEALEO

Pokémon Data

Ball Roll Pokémon

TYPE	Ice
	Water
ABILITIES	Thick Fat
	Ice Body
HEIGHT	3´07″
WEIGHT	193.1 lbs

National Pokédex No.
364

Description

Sealeo likes to spin things on its nose. This is how it differentiates between things it likes and dislikes, going by the smells and textures of the objects.

Special Moves

Aurora Beam, Hail, Rest, Snore

EVOLUTION

Spheal → Sealeo → Walrein

WALREIN

1-
49

50-
99

100-
149

150-
199

200-
249

250-
299

300-
349

350-
399

400-
449

450-
491

Pokémon Data

Ice Break Pokémon

TYPE	Ice
	Water
ABILITIES	Thick Fat
	Ice Body
HEIGHT	4′07″
WEIGHT	332.0 lbs

Description

Walrein swims the icy seas while breaking apart the ice with its two large tusks. Its thick layer of fat fends off both the cold and enemy attacks.

National Pokédex No.

365

Special Moves

Ice Fang, Blizzard, Sheer Cold

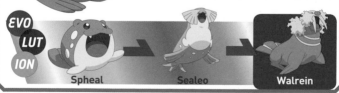

EVO LUT ION

Spheal ▸ Sealeo ▸ Walrein

123

CLAMPERL

Pokémon Data

Bivalve Pokémon	
TYPE	Water ...
ABILITIES	Shell Armor ...
HEIGHT	1´04˝
WEIGHT	115.7 lbs

National Pokédex No.
366

Description

As Clamperl grows, it's protected by its hard shell. The single pearl it creates in its lifetime supposedly has properties that can strengthen psychic powers.

Special Moves

Clamp, Water Gun, Iron Defense

EVOLUTION

Clamperl

Gorebyss   **Huntail**

HUNTAIL

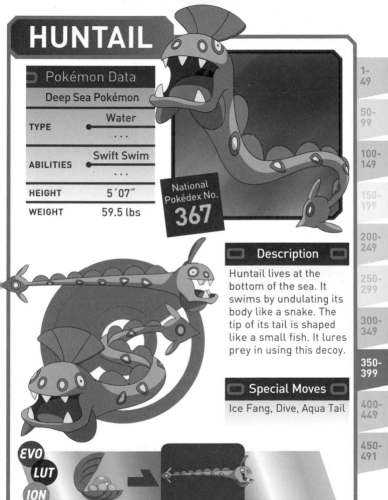

Pokémon Data

Deep Sea Pokémon

TYPE	Water
	. . .
ABILITIES	Swift Swim
	. . .
HEIGHT	5´07˝
WEIGHT	59.5 lbs

National Pokédex No.
367

1-49
50-99
100-149
150-199
200-249
250-299
300-349
350-399
400-449
450-491

Description

Huntail lives at the bottom of the sea. It swims by undulating its body like a snake. The tip of its tail is shaped like a small fish. It lures prey in using this decoy.

Special Moves

Ice Fang, Dive, Aqua Tail

EVO LUT ION

Clamperl → Huntail

125

GOREBYSS

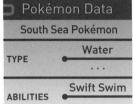

Pokémon Data

South Sea Pokémon

TYPE	Water
	. . .
ABILITIES	Swift Swim
	. . .
HEIGHT	5'11"
WEIGHT	49.8 lbs

Description

Gorebyss lives in the southern seas. Its body can withstand the pressure of the depths, and a minor attack will not injure it in the least.

National Pokédex No.
368

Special Moves

Aqua Ring, Dive, Hydro Pump

EVO LUT ION

Clamperl → Gorebyss

RELICANTH

Pokémon Data

Longevity Pokémon

TYPE	Water
	Rock
ABILITIES	Swift Swim
	Rock Head
HEIGHT	3′03″
WEIGHT	51.6 lbs

Description

Relicanth has lived in the ocean depths for over a hundred million years without ever changing form. Its rock-hard scales are able to withstand extreme pressure.

Special Moves

Ancient Power, Rest, Hydro Pump

National Pokédex No.
369

EVOLUTION

Relicanth

Does not Evolve

1-49
50-99
100-149
150-199
200-249
250-299
300-349
350-399
400-449
450-491

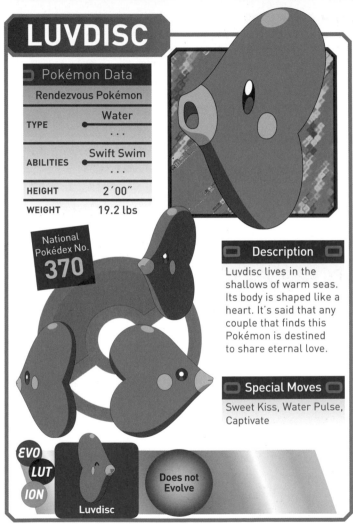

LUVDISC

Pokémon Data

Rendezvous Pokémon

TYPE	Water
	...
ABILITIES	Swift Swim
	...
HEIGHT	2′00″
WEIGHT	19.2 lbs

National Pokédex No.

370

Description

Luvdisc lives in the shallows of warm seas. Its body is shaped like a heart. It's said that any couple that finds this Pokémon is destined to share eternal love.

Special Moves

Sweet Kiss, Water Pulse, Captivate

EVO
LUT
ION

Luvdisc

Does not Evolve

BAGON

Pokémon Data

Rock Head Pokémon

TYPE	Dragon . . .
ABILITIES	Rock Head . . .
HEIGHT	2´00˝
WEIGHT	92.8 lbs

National Pokédex No.
371

Description

Bagon's dream is to fly the skies, and so it practices every day by jumping off cliffs. But since it still cannot fly, it lets out its frustration by crushing boulders with its hard head.

Special Moves

Rage, Headbutt, Focus Energy, Ember

EVO
LUT
ION

Bagon → Shelgon → Salamence

1-49
50-99
100-149
150-199
200-249
250-299
300-349
350-399
400-449
450-491

SHELGON

Pokémon Data

Endurance Pokémon

TYPE	Dragon . . .
ABILITIES	Rock Head . . .
HEIGHT	3´07˝
WEIGHT	243.6 lbs

Description

Within its hard shell, where it's busy creating a new body, it waits patiently to Evolve. As soon as it's ready to Evolve, the shell peels right off.

National Pokédex No.

372

Special Moves

Focus Energy, Protect, Dragon Breath

EVO LUT ION

  Bagon → Shelgon → Salamence

SALAMENCE

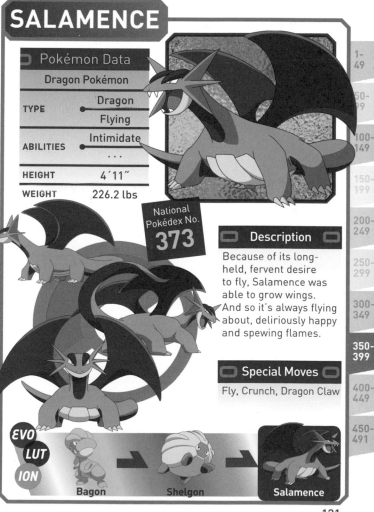

Pokémon Data

Dragon Pokémon

TYPE	Dragon
	Flying
ABILITIES	Intimidate
	. . .
HEIGHT	4′11″
WEIGHT	226.2 lbs

National Pokédex No.
373

Description

Because of its long-held, fervent desire to fly, Salamence was able to grow wings. And so it's always flying about, deliriously happy and spewing flames.

Special Moves

Fly, Crunch, Dragon Claw

EVO LUT ION

Bagon ▶ Shelgon ▶ Salamence

1–49
50–99
100–149
150–199
200–249
250–299
300–349
350–399
400–449
450–491

BELDUM

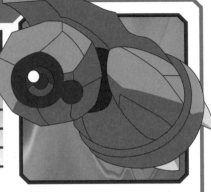

Pokémon Data

Iron Ball Pokémon

TYPE	Steel
	Psychic
ABILITIES	Clear Body
	. . .
HEIGHT	2′00″
WEIGHT	209.9 lbs

National Pokédex No.
374

Description

Beldum uses magnetic force to stay afloat. Instead of blood, it has a magnetic field flowing within its body. They communicate with magnetic pulses.

Special Moves

Take Down

EVOLUTION

Beldum   Metang   Metagross

METANG

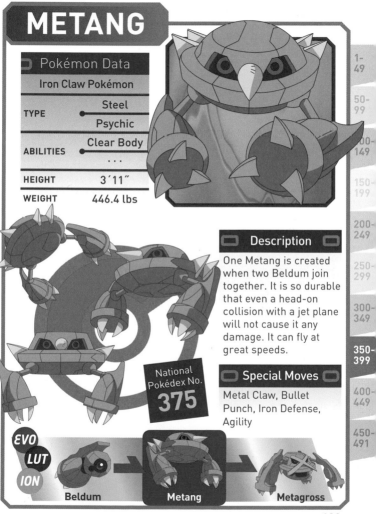

Pokémon Data

Iron Claw Pokémon

TYPE	Steel
	Psychic
ABILITIES	Clear Body
	. . .
HEIGHT	3´11˝
WEIGHT	446.4 lbs

1-
49

50-
99

00-
149

150-
199

200-
249

250-
299

300-
349

350-
399

400-
449

450-
491

Description

One Metang is created when two Beldum join together. It is so durable that even a head-on collision with a jet plane will not cause it any damage. It can fly at great speeds.

National Pokédex No.

375

Special Moves

Metal Claw, Bullet Punch, Iron Defense, Agility

EVO
LUT
ION

Beldum → Metang → Metagross

133

METAGROSS

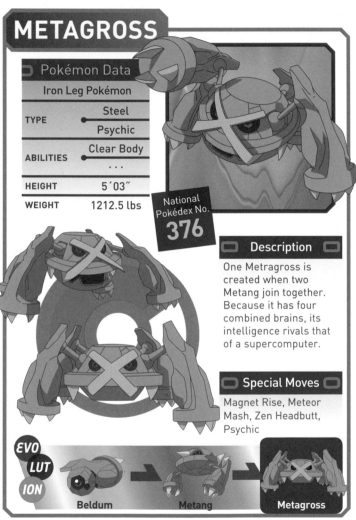

Pokémon Data

Iron Leg Pokémon

TYPE	Steel
	Psychic
ABILITIES	Clear Body
	. . .
HEIGHT	5′03″
WEIGHT	1212.5 lbs

National Pokédex No.
376

Description

One Metragross is created when two Metang join together. Because it has four combined brains, its intelligence rivals that of a supercomputer.

Special Moves

Magnet Rise, Meteor Mash, Zen Headbutt, Psychic

EVOLUTION

Beldum ➤ Metang ➤ Metagross

REGIROCK

Pokémon Data

Rock Peak Pokémon

TYPE	Rock . . .
ABILITIES	Clear Body . . .
HEIGHT	5´07˝
WEIGHT	507.1 lbs

Description

Regirock is made entirely of boulders. Without a brain or a heart, it is a mystery even for modern science. When its body is damaged, it repairs itself with rocks.

Special Moves

Superpower, Iron Defense, Stone Edge

National Pokédex No.
377

EVO LUT ION

Regirock

Does not Evolve

1-49

50-99

100-149

150-199

200-249

250-299

300-349

350-399

400-449

450-491

REGICE

Pokémon Data

Iceberg Pokémon

TYPE	Ice
	. . .
ABILITIES	Clear Body
	. . .
HEIGHT	5´11˝
WEIGHT	385.8 lbs

Description

Regice protects itself in an envelope of cold air held at -328ºF. Its body was created back during the last Ice Age. Not even lava can melt it.

National Pokédex No.
378

Special Moves

Icy Wind, Superpower, Ice Beam

EVO LUT ION

Regice

Does not Evolve

REGISTEEL

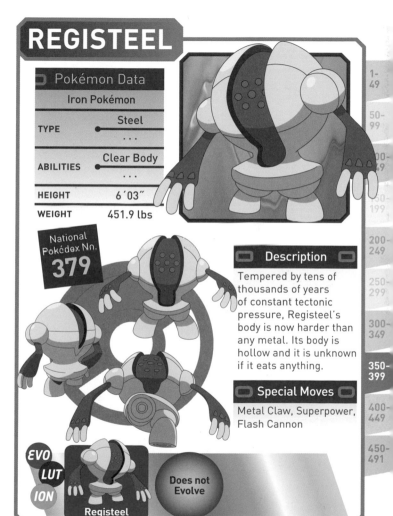

Pokémon Data

Iron Pokémon

TYPE	Steel
	...
ABILITIES	Clear Body
	...
HEIGHT	6′03″
WEIGHT	451.9 lbs

National Pokédex No.
379

Description

Tempered by tens of thousands of years of constant tectonic pressure, Registeel's body is now harder than any metal. Its body is hollow and it is unknown if it eats anything.

Special Moves

Metal Claw, Superpower, Flash Cannon

EVOLUTION

Registeel — Does not Evolve

1-49
50-99
100-149
150-199
200-249
250-299
300-349
350-399
400-449
450-491

LATIAS

Pokémon Data

Eon Pokémon

TYPE	Dragon
	Psychic
ABILITIES	Levitate
	...
HEIGHT	4′07″
WEIGHT	88.2 lbs

Description

Latias can read the hearts of humans, and because of its high intelligence it can also understand human speech. The specialized feathers that cover its body refract light.

National Pokédex No.
380

Special Moves

Mist Ball, Dragon Pulse, Charm, Psychic

EVO LUT ION

Latias

Does not Evolve

LATIOS

Pokémon Data

Eon Pokémon

TYPE	Dragon
	Psychic
ABILITIES	Levitate
	. . .
HEIGHT	6´07˝
WEIGHT	132.3 lbs

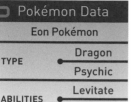

Description

Latios becomes attached only to those with kind hearts. One Latios can transmit to another an image of what it sees or what it is thinking. It can fly faster than a jet plane.

National Pokédex No.
381

Special Moves

Refresh, Luster Purge, Dragon Pulse

EVO
LUT
ION

Latios

Does not Evolve

1-49
50-99
100-149
150-199
200-249
250-299
300-349
350-399
400-449
450-491

KYOGRE

Pokémon Data

Sea Basin Pokémon

TYPE	Water
	. . .
ABILITIES	Drizzle
	. . .
HEIGHT	14´09″
WEIGHT	776.0 lbs

National Pokédex No.
382

Description

It is said that Kyogre, the Pokémon that controls water, made the oceans larger by blanketing the land with heavy downpours and massive wave surges.

Special Moves

Hydro Pump, Sheer Cold, Water Spout

EVO LUT ION

Kyogre

Does not Evolve

GROUDON

Pokémon Data

Continent Pokémon

TYPE	Ground
	...
ABILITIES	Drought
	...
HEIGHT	11´06″
WEIGHT	2094.4 lbs

1-49

50-99

100-149

150-199

200-249

250-299

300-349

350-399

400-449

450-491

Description

Ever since its battle against Kyogre, it has been sleeping in the magma deep under the ground. Groudon has the power to evaporate water through light and heat.

National Pokédex No.
383

Special Moves

Bulk Up, Fire Blast, Earth Power

EVO LUT ION

Groudon

Does not Evolve

RAYQUAZA

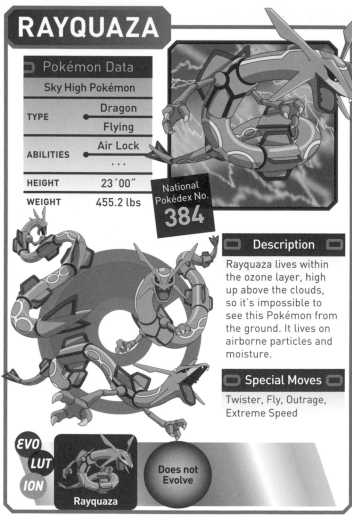

Pokémon Data

Sky High Pokémon

TYPE	Dragon
	Flying
ABILITIES	Air Lock
	. . .
HEIGHT	23´00˝
WEIGHT	455.2 lbs

National Pokédex No.
384

Description

Rayquaza lives within the ozone layer, high up above the clouds, so it's impossible to see this Pokémon from the ground. It lives on airborne particles and moisture.

Special Moves

Twister, Fly, Outrage, Extreme Speed

EVO LUT ION

Rayquaza

Does not Evolve

JIRACHI

Pokémon Data

Wish Pokémon

TYPE	Steel
	Psychic
ABILITIES	Serene Grace
	. . .
HEIGHT	1´00˝
WEIGHT	2.4 lbs

National Pokédex No.
385

Description

Jirachi is awake for only seven days every thousand years. It is said to have the power to grant any wish during this time.

Special Moves

Rest, Healing Wish, Doom Desire

EVO LUT ION

Jirachi

Does not Evolve

1-49
50-99
100-149
150-199
200-249
250-299
300-349
350-399
400-449
450-491

DEOXYS

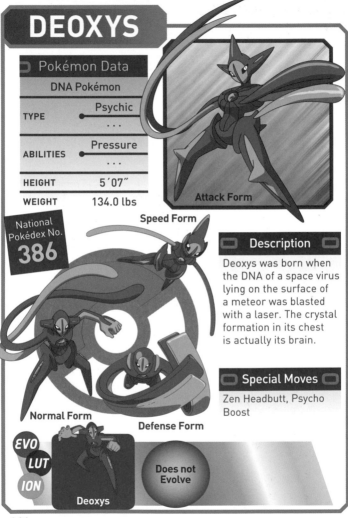

Pokémon Data

DNA Pokémon

TYPE	Psychic
	...
ABILITIES	Pressure
	...
HEIGHT	5´07˝
WEIGHT	134.0 lbs

Attack Form

Speed Form

National Pokédex No. **386**

Normal Form

Defense Form

Description

Deoxys was born when the DNA of a space virus lying on the surface of a meteor was blasted with a laser. The crystal formation in its chest is actually its brain.

Special Moves

Zen Headbutt, Psycho Boost

EVO LUT ION

Deoxys

Does not Evolve

TURTWIG

Pokémon Data

Tiny Leaf Pokémon

TYPE	Grass
	...
ABILITIES	Overgrow
	...
HEIGHT	1'04"
WEIGHT	22.5 lbs

National Pokédex No. **387**

Description

Turwig creates oxygen by absorbing sunlight with its whole body. The shell on its back is made of dirt and becomes harder when it drinks water.

Special Moves

Tackle, Withdraw, Razor Leaf

EVO LUT ION

Turtwig → Grotle → Torterra

1-49
50-99
100-149
150-199
200-249
250-299
300-349
350-399
400-449
450-491

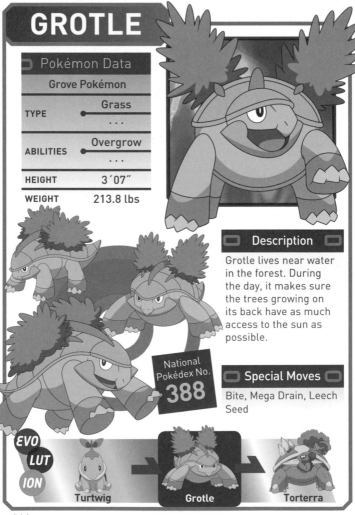

GROTLE

Pokémon Data

Grove Pokémon

TYPE	Grass
	. . .
ABILITIES	Overgrow
	. . .
HEIGHT	3´07˝
WEIGHT	213.8 lbs

Description

Grotle lives near water in the forest. During the day, it makes sure the trees growing on its back have as much access to the sun as possible.

National Pokédex No.

388

Special Moves

Bite, Mega Drain, Leech Seed

EVO LUT ION

Turtwig → Grotle → Torterra

146

TORTERRA

Pokémon Data

Continent Pokémon

TYPE	Grass
	Ground
ABILITIES	Overgrow
	. . .
HEIGHT	7′03″
WEIGHT	683.4 lbs

Description

If Torterra stays still for any length of time, small Pokémon come and create nests on its back. When it moves in search of water, it looks like a walking forest.

National Pokédex No. **389**

Special Moves

Earthquake, Giga Drain, Wood Hammer, Crunch

EVO LUT ION

Turtwig ▶ Grotle ▶ Torterra

1-49
50-99
100-149
150-199
200-249
250-299
300-349
350-399
400-449
450-491

CHIMCHAR

Pokémon Data

Chimp Pokémon

TYPE	Fire
	. . .
ABILITIES	Blaze
	. . .
HEIGHT	1´08˝
WEIGHT	13.7 lbs

National
Pokédex No.
390

Description

Chimchar lives on rocky crags and can easily climb any cliff. The flame on its tail is fueled by gas created within its abdomen and cannot be doused even by rain.

Special Moves

Scratch, Ember, Taunt, Fury Swipes

EVO LUT ION

Chimchar ▶ Monferno ▶ Infernape

MONFERNO

Pokémon Data

Playful Pokémon

TYPE	Fire
	Fighting
ABILITIES	Blaze
	. . .
HEIGHT	2′11″
WEIGHT	48.5 lbs

National Pokédex No. **391**

1–49

50–99

100–149

150–199

200–249

250–299

300–349

350–399

400–449

450–491

Description

Monferno creates aerial attacks by rebounding off ceilings and walls. To intimidate its opponent, it will make its body seem larger by suddenly increasing the size of the flame on its tail.

Special Moves

Mach Punch, Flame Wheel, Fury Swipes

EVO LUT ION

Chimchar   Monferno   Infernape

INFERNAPE

Pokémon Data

Flame Pokémon	
TYPE	Fire
	Fighting
ABILITIES	Blaze
	...
HEIGHT	3´11″
WEIGHT	121.3 lbs

National Pokédex No.
392

Description

Infernape has extremely fast moves and its very own fighting technique. Its personality is as fiery as the flames on its head. These flames can't be extinguished as long as it's alive.

Special Moves

Close Combat, Calm Mind, Flare Blitz

EVO LUT ION

Chimchar → Monferno → Infernape

150

PIPLUP

Pokémon Data

Penguin Pokémon

TYPE	Water
	. . .
ABILITIES	Torrent
	. . .
HEIGHT	1´04"
WEIGHT	11.5 lbs

National Pokédex No.
393

Description

Piplup lives on the coasts of cold countries. It's a good swimmer and can stay underwater for up to ten minutes. It also has a lot of pride and will never ask a human for food.

Special Moves

Growl, Bubble, Water Sport, Peck

EVOLUTION

Piplup → Prinplup → Empoleon

1-49
50-99
100-149
150-199
200-249
250-299
300-349
350-399
400-449
450-491

PRINPLUP

Pokémon Data

Penguin Pokémon

TYPE	Water
	. . .
ABILITIES	Torrent
	. . .
HEIGHT	2´07″
WEIGHT	50.7 lbs

National Pokédex No.
394

Description

Prinplup survives by hunting prey in freezing oceans. Each Prinplup believes it is the most important one. A single blow from its wings is powerful enough to break a large tree in two.

Special Moves

Brine, Bubble Beam, Fury Attack

EVOLUTION

Piplup → Prinplup → Empoleon

EMPOLEON

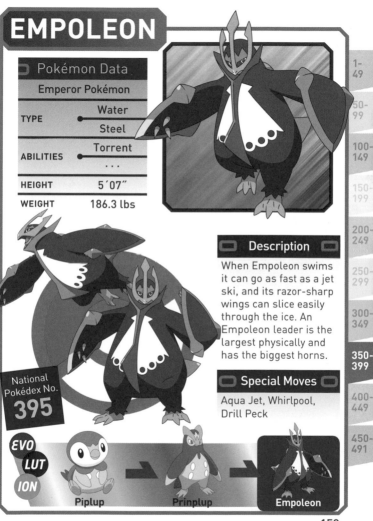

Pokémon Data

Emperor Pokémon

TYPE	Water
	Steel
ABILITIES	Torrent
	. . .
HEIGHT	5´07˝
WEIGHT	186.3 lbs

Description

When Empoleon swims it can go as fast as a jet ski, and its razor-sharp wings can slice easily through the ice. An Empoleon leader is the largest physically and has the biggest horns.

Special Moves

Aqua Jet, Whirlpool, Drill Peck

National Pokédex No.
395

EVO LUT ION

Piplup → Prinplup → Empoleon

1-49
50-99
100-149
150-199
200-249
250-299
300-349
350-399
400-449
450-491

STARLY

Pokémon Data

Starling Pokémon

TYPE	Normal
	Flying
ABILITIES	Keen Eye
	. . .
HEIGHT	1´00″
WEIGHT	4.4 lbs

Description

Although Starly are small, their wings are very powerful. They can usually be found in large flocks and can be hard to detect when alone.

National Pokédex No.
396

Special Moves

Growl, Quick Attack, Wing Attack

EVO LUT ION

Starly ➤ Staravia ➤ Staraptor

STARAVIA

Pokémon Data

Starling Pokémon

TYPE	Normal
	Flying
ABILITIES	Intimidate
	. . .
HEIGHT	2′00″
WEIGHT	34.2 lbs

National Pokédex No.
397

Description

Staravia fly over forests and plains in search of food. They travel in large flocks, and when two different flocks encounter one another a territorial fight will usually follow.

Special Moves

Growl, Quick Attack, Wing Attack

1-49
50-99
100-149
150-199
200-249
250-299
300-349
350-399
400-449
450-491

EVO LUT ION

Starly   Staravia   Staraptor

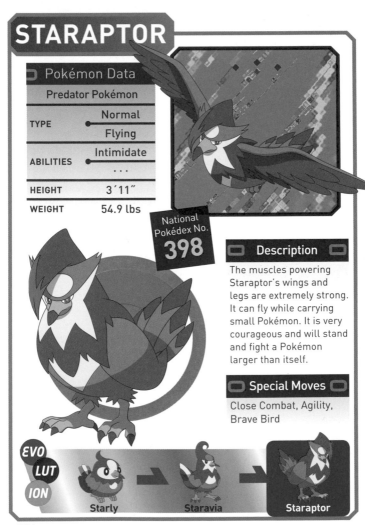

STARAPTOR

Pokémon Data

Predator Pokémon

TYPE	Normal
	Flying
ABILITIES	Intimidate
	. . .
HEIGHT	3′11″
WEIGHT	54.9 lbs

National Pokédex No.
398

Description

The muscles powering Staraptor's wings and legs are extremely strong. It can fly while carrying small Pokémon. It is very courageous and will stand and fight a Pokémon larger than itself.

Special Moves

Close Combat, Agility, Brave Bird

EVOLUTION

Starly → Staravia → Staraptor

BIDOOF

Pokémon Data

Plump Mouse Pokémon

TYPE	Normal
	. . .
ABILITIES	Simple
	Unaware
HEIGHT	1´08˝
WEIGHT	44.1 lbs

Description

Bidoof pares down its front teeth by constantly gnawing on trees and stones. It has nerves of steel: nothing seems to be able to startle it. Despite appearances, it can move very quickly.

Special Moves

Tackle, Growl, Defense Curl, Rollout

National Pokédex No.
399

1-49
50-99
100-149
150-199
200-249
250-299
300-349
350-399
400-449
450-491

EVO LUT ION

Bidoof → Bibarel

BIBAREL

Pokémon Data

Beaver Pokémon

TYPE	Normal
	Water
ABILITIES	Simple
	Unaware
HEIGHT	3´03″
WEIGHT	69.4 lbs

National Pokédex No.
400

Description

Bibarel creates its nest by damming up a river with trees and mud. Although slow-moving on land, its speed in the water rivals that of a Feebas.

Special Moves

Take Down, Hyper Fang, Superpower

EVO LUT ION

Bidoof

Bibarel

KRICKETOT

Pokémon Data

Cricket Pokémon

TYPE	Bug
	. . .
ABILITIES	Shed Skin
	. . .
HEIGHT	1′00″
WEIGHT	4.9 lbs

National Pokédex No.
401

Description

It creates sound by shaking its head back and forth, which causes its antennae to rub together. Kricketot use these sounds to communicate with one another.

Special Moves

Growl, Bide

EVOLUTION

Kricketot

Kricketune

1-49
50-99
100-149
150-199
200-249
250-299
300-349
350-399
400-449
450-491

KRICKETUNE

Pokémon Data

Cricket Pokémon

TYPE	Bug
	. . .
ABILITIES	Swarm
	. . .
HEIGHT	3´03″
WEIGHT	56.2 lbs

National Pokédex No. **402**

Description

It sings by rubbing its arms back and forth against one another in front of its body. Kricketune expresses itself through melodies that it creates as it experiences things.

Special Moves

X-Scissor, Screech, Perish Song

 EVO LUT ION

 Kricketot → **Kricketune**

SHINX

Pokémon Data

Flash Pokémon

TYPE	Electric
	. . .
ABILITIES	Rivalry
	Intimidate
HEIGHT	1´08˝
WEIGHT	20.9 lbs

National Pokédex No.

403

1–49

50–99

100–149

150–199

200–249

250–299

300–349

350–399

400–449

450–491

Description

When Shinx is cornered, the fur on its whole body flares brightly. It makes its escape while its opponent is blinded by the light.

Special Moves

Tackle, Leer, Charge

EVO LUT ION

Shinx   Luxio   Luxray

LUXIO

Pokémon Data

Spark Pokémon	
TYPE	Electric . . .
ABILITIES	Rivalry Intimidate
HEIGHT	2´11˝
WEIGHT	67.2 lbs

National Pokédex No.
404

Description

The surge of electricity Luxio releases through its claws is so powerful that just one strike can fell an opponent. They communicate with each other using rhythmic electrical pulses.

Special Moves

Leer, Spark, Roar, Swagger

EVO LUT ION

Shinx

Luxio

Luxray

LUXRAY

Pokémon Data

Gleam Eyes Pokémon

TYPE	Electric
	...
ABILITIES	Rivalry
	Intimidate
HEIGHT	4′07″
WEIGHT	92.6 lbs

National Pokédex No.
405

1-49
50-99
100-149
150-199
200-249
250-299
300-349
350-399
400-449
450-491

Description

When Luxray's golden eyes are shining, it's using a power that enables it to see through anything. Then it will quickly find and capture even hidden prey.

Special Moves

Crunch, Thunder Fang, Discharge

EVO LUT ION

Shinx → Luxio → Luxray

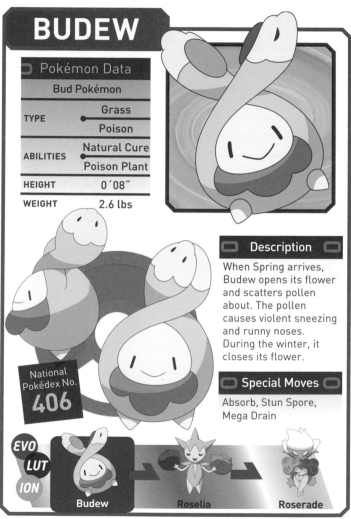

BUDEW

Pokémon Data

Bud Pokémon

TYPE	Grass
	Poison
ABILITIES	Natural Cure
	Poison Plant
HEIGHT	0´08˝
WEIGHT	2.6 lbs

National Pokédex No.
406

Description

When Spring arrives, Budew opens its flower and scatters pollen about. The pollen causes violent sneezing and runny noses. During the winter, it closes its flower.

Special Moves

Absorb, Stun Spore, Mega Drain

EVOLUTION

Budew → Roselia → Roserade

ROSERADE

Pokémon Data

Bouquet Pokémon

TYPE	Grass
	Poison
ABILITIES	Natural Cure
	Poison Point
HEIGHT	2′11″
WEIGHT	32.0 lbs

National Pokédex No.
407

Description

Hidden within the flower bouquets in both hands are vine whips covered with poison thorns. With a dancer's grace, Roserade will attack opponents with these whips.

Special Moves

Weather Ball, Poison Sting, Magical Leaf

EVO LUT ION

Budew → Roselia → Roserade

1-49
50-99
100-149
150-199
200-249
250-299
300-349
350-399
400-449
450-491

CRANIDOS

Pokémon Data

Head Butt Pokémon

TYPE	Rock
	...
ABILITIES	Mold Breaker
	...
HEIGHT	2´11″
WEIGHT	69.4 lbs

National Pokédex No.
408

Description

A Pokémon resurrected from a fossil that resembled an iron ball. A hundred million years ago, Cranidos lived in the forests and captured prey by using headbutts.

Special Moves

Headbutt, Focus Energy, Take Down, Assurance

EVO LUT ION

Cranidos   Rampardos

RAMPARDOS

Pokémon Data

Head Butt Pokémon

TYPE	Rock
	...
ABILITIES	Mold Breaker
	...
HEIGHT	5´03˝
WEIGHT	226.0 lbs

National Pokédex No.
409

Description

Rampardos's head is harder than steel, and it is very skilled in using a headbutt attack. Once it sights its opponent, it will attack fiercely, ripping up the landscape along the way.

Special Moves

Endeavor, Screech, Head Smash

EVO LUT ION

Cranidos → Rampardos

9
50-99
100-149
150-199
200-249
250-299
300-349
350-399
400-449
450-491

SHIELDON

Pokémon Data

Shield Pokémon	
TYPE	Rock
	Steel
ABILITIES	Sturdy
	. . .
HEIGHT	1´08˝
WEIGHT	125.7 lbs

National Pokédex No.
410

Description

Shieldon lived in ancient forests a hundred million years ago. It polishes the hard shield around its head by rubbing it against trees. It is weak against attacks from behind.

Special Moves

Take Down, Iron Defense, Ancient Power

EVOLUTION

Shieldon

Bastiodon

BASTIODON

1–
49

50–
99

100–
149

150–
199

200–
249

250–
299

300–
349

350–
399

400–
449

450–
491

Pokémon Data

Shield Pokémon	
TYPE	Rock
	Steel
ABILITIES	Sturdy
	. . .
HEIGHT	4´03˝
WEIGHT	329.6 lbs

National Pokédex No.
411

Description

When attacked by an enemy, Bastiodon uses its shield face as a protective barrier. It can repel any frontal attack. It is a peaceful Pokémon, and lives on grass and berries.

Special Moves

Protect, Metal Burst, Iron Head

EVOLUTION

Shieldon → Bastiodon

BURMY

Pokémon Data

Bagworm Pokémon

TYPE	Bug
	. . .
ABILITIES	Shed Skin
	. . .
HEIGHT	0´08˝
WEIGHT	7.5 lbs

Plant Cloak

National Pokédex No.
412

Trash Cloak

Sandy Cloak

Description

Burmy creates a cloak out of small twigs and fallen leaves in order to protect itself from the cold. If its cloak is damaged during battle, it can easily create another one using any materials at hand.

Special Moves

Protect, Tackle, Hidden Power

EVO LUT ION

Burmy → Wormadam, Mothim

WORMADAM
(Plant Cloak)

Pokémon Data

Bagworm Pokémon

TYPE	Bug
	Grass
ABILITIES	Anticipation
	. . .
HEIGHT	1´08″
WEIGHT	14.3 lbs

National Pokédex No.
413

Description

When a Burmy (Plant Cloak) Evolves, it becomes a Wormadam (Plant Cloak). Because the cloak fuses with its body when it Evolves, a Wormadam can never remove its cloak.

Special Moves

Razor Leaf, Captivate, Leaf Storm

EVO LUT ION

Burmy → Wormadam

1-49
50-99
100-149
150-199
200-249
250-299
300-349
350-399
400-449
450-491

WORMADAM
(Sandy Cloak)

Pokémon Data

Bagworm Pokémon	
TYPE	Bug
	Ground
ABILITIES	Anticipation
	. . .
HEIGHT	1´08˝
WEIGHT	14.3 lbs

National Pokédex No.
413

Description

When a Burmy (Sandy Cloak) Evolves, it becomes a Wormadam (Sandy Cloak). Because the cloak fuses with its body when it Evolves, a Wormadam can never remove its cloak.

Special Moves

Rock Blast, Harden, Fissure

EVO LUT ION

Burmy → Wormadam

WORMADAM
(Trash Cloak)

Pokémon Data

Bagworm Pokémon	
TYPE	Bug
	Steel
ABILITIES	Anticipation
	. . .
HEIGHT	1´08˝
WEIGHT	14.3 lbs

National Pokédex No.
413

Description

When a Burmy (Trash Cloak) Evolves, it becomes a Wormadam (Trash Cloak). Because the cloak fuses with its body when it Evolves, a Wormadam can never remove its cloak.

Special Moves

Mirror Shot, Attract, Iron Head

EVOLUTION

Burmy

Wormadam

1-49
50-99
100-149
150-199
200-249
250-299
300-349
350-399
400-449
450-491

MOTHIM

Pokémon Data

Moth Pokémon

TYPE	Bug
	Flying
ABILITIES	Swarm
	...
HEIGHT	2´11″
WEIGHT	51.4 lbs

Description

Mothim doesn't have a nest, and instead flitters about the hills and fields in search of honey. It's been known to steal the honey collected by Combee.

National Pokédex No. **414**

Special Moves

Gust, Camouflage, Silver Wind

EVO LUT ION

Burmy   Mothim

COMBEE

Pokémon Data

Tiny Bee Pokémon

TYPE	Bug
	Flying
ABILITIES	Honey Gather
	. . .
HEIGHT	1´00˝
WEIGHT	12.1 lbs

National Pokédex No.
415

Description

A Combee is three Pokémon sharing one body. They collect honey and bring it back to the hive for their Vespiquen. At night, when going to sleep, they all stack together.

Special Moves

Sweet Scent, Gust

EVO LUT ION

Combee → Vespiquen

1–49
50–99
100–149
150–199
200–249
250–299
300–349
350–399
400–449
450–491

175

VESPIQUEN

Pokémon Data

Beehive Pokémon	
TYPE	Bug
	Flying
ABILITIES	Pressure
	. . .
HEIGHT	3′11″
WEIGHT	84.9 lbs

National Pokédex No. **416**

Description

The six cells in Vespiquen's abdomen serve as a nest for its children. It feeds them honey collected by Combee. When in danger, its children fly out of the combs.

Special Moves

Defend Order, Swagger, Heal Order, Attack Order

EVOLUTION

Combee

Vespiquen

176

PACHIRISU

Pokémon Data

EleSquirrel Pokémon

TYPE	Electric
	. . .
ABILITIES	Run Away
	Pickup
HEIGHT	1´04″
WEIGHT	8.6 lbs

National Pokédex No. **417**

Description

Pachirisu stashes its favorite berries together with fur balls crackling with static charge. It generates electricity in the pouches on its cheeks and shoots charges from its tail.

Special Moves

Quick Attack, Spark, Swift, Super Fang

EVO LUT ION

Pachirisu

Does not Evolve

1-49
50-99
100-149
150-199
200-249
250-299
300-349
350-399
400-449
450-491

BUIZEL

Pokémon Data

Sea Weasel Pokémon

TYPE	Water
	. . .
ABILITIES	Swift Swim
	. . .
HEIGHT	2´04″
WEIGHT	65.0 lbs

National Pokédex No.
418

Description

Buizel floats in water by inflating the floatation ring around its neck and deflates the ring when it needs to dive. It swims by corkscrewing its two tails.

Special Moves

Pursuit, Swift, Aqua Jet

 EVO LUT ION

 Buizel

 Floatzel

FLOATZEL

Pokémon Data

Sea Weasel Pokémon

TYPE	Water …
ABILITIES	Swift Swim …
HEIGHT	3′07″
WEIGHT	73.9 lbs

National Pokédex No.
419

Description

Its floatation sac evolved as it pursued aquatic prey. The sac can even support people like a life raft, and Floatzel frequently aids humans in rescuing drowning victims.

Special Moves

Crunch, Aqua Jet, Whirlpool

EVO LUT ION

Buizel → Floatzel

1-49
50-99
100-149
150-199
200-249
250-299
300-349
350-399
400-449
450-491

179

CHERUBI

Pokémon Data

Cherry Pokémon

TYPE	Grass
	...
ABILITIES	Chlorophyll
	...
HEIGHT	1´04˝
WEIGHT	7.3 lbs

National Pokédex No.

420

Description

Nutrients necessary for Cherubi's Evolution are packed into the smaller sphere, which is said to be very sweet. The sphere shrivels up after the nutrients have been all used up.

Special Moves

Tackle, Leech Seed, Helping Hand

EVO LUT ION

Cherubi

Cherrim

CHERRIM

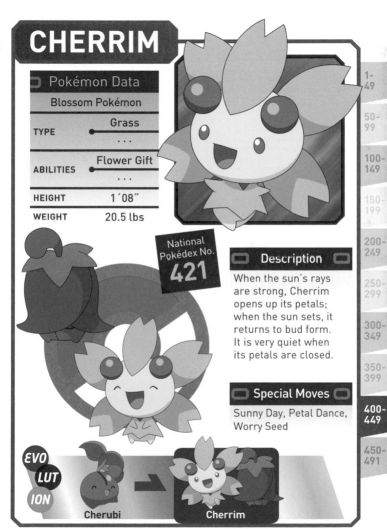

Pokémon Data

Blossom Pokémon

TYPE	Grass
	...
ABILITIES	Flower Gift
	...
HEIGHT	1´08˝
WEIGHT	20.5 lbs

National Pokédex No.
421

Description

When the sun's rays are strong, Cherrim opens up its petals; when the sun sets, it returns to bud form. It is very quiet when its petals are closed.

Special Moves

Sunny Day, Petal Dance, Worry Seed

EVO LUT ION

Cherubi → Cherrim

1-49
50-99
100-149
150-199
200-249
250-299
300-349
350-399
400-449
450-491

SHELLOS

Pokémon Data

Sea Slug Pokémon	
TYPE	Water
	. . .
ABILITIES	Sticky Hold
	Storm Drain
HEIGHT	1´00˝
WEIGHT	13.9 lbs

National Pokédex No. **422**

Description

Shellos live along the seashore. The two types found on the eastern shore of Sinnoh have a different shape and color than those found on the western shore.

Special Moves

Mud Sport, Harden, Water Pulse

EVO LUT ION

Shellos

Gastrodon

GASTRODON

Pokémon Data

Sea Slug Pokémon	
TYPE	Water
	Ground
ABILITIES	Sticky Hold
	Storm Drain
HEIGHT	2′11″
WEIGHT	65.9 lbs

National Pokédex No.
423

Description

Gastrodon lives in the shallows of the sea. Its body is boneless and pliable, and even if a part of it gets torn off, it can easily be regrown.

Special Moves

Body Slam, Muddy Water, Recover

EVO
LUT
ION

Shellos

Gastrodon

1-49
50-99
100-149
150-199
200-249
250-299
300-349
350-399
400-449
450-491

AMBIPOM

Pokémon Data

Long Tail Pokémon

TYPE	Normal
	...
ABILITIES	Technician
	Pickup
HEIGHT	3´11″
WEIGHT	44.8 lbs

National Pokédex No.

424

Description

It rarely uses its arms and instead uses its two tails to deftly crack nuts to eat. Ambipom often link their tails together as a sign of friendship.

Special Moves

Double Hit, Nasty Plot, Fling

EVOLUTION

Aipom → Ambipom

DRIFLOON

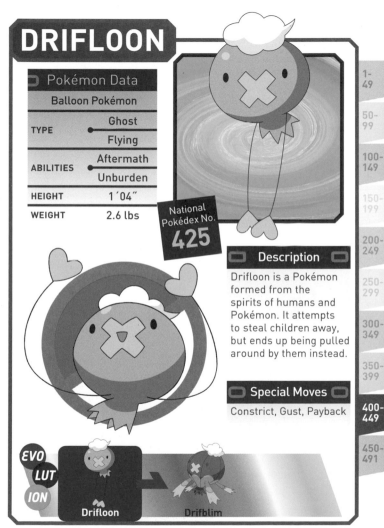

Pokémon Data

Balloon Pokémon

TYPE	Ghost
	Flying
ABILITIES	Aftermath
	Unburden
HEIGHT	1´04˝
WEIGHT	2.6 lbs

National Pokédex No. **425**

Description

Drifloon is a Pokémon formed from the spirits of humans and Pokémon. It attempts to steal children away, but ends up being pulled around by them instead.

Special Moves

Constrict, Gust, Payback

EVOLUTION

Drifloon → Drifblim

1-49
50-99
100-149
150-199
200-249
250-299
300-349
350-399
400-449
450-491

DRIFBLIM

Pokémon Data

Blimp Pokémon

TYPE	Ghost
	Flying
ABILITIES	Aftermath
	Unburden
HEIGHT	3´11˝
WEIGHT	33.1 lbs

National Pokédex No.
426

Description

Large groups of Drifblim can be seen flying off at sunset, but no one knows their destination. They can fly while carrying others, but the destination depends on the wind.

Special Moves

Ominous Wind, Shadow Ball, Explosion

EVOLUTION

Drifloon → Drifblim

BUNEARY

Pokémon Data

Rabbit Pokémon

TYPE	Normal
	. . .
ABILITIES	Run Away
	Klutz
HEIGHT	1´04˝
WEIGHT	12.1 lbs

National Pokédex No.
427

Description

Buneary smacks its opponent by whipping out its curled-up ears. It extends both ears up only when it senses danger. On cold nights, it curls around itself to sleep.

Special Moves

Pound, Defense Curl, Quick Attack

EVOLUTION

Buneary → Lopunny

1-49
50-99
100-149
150-199
200-249
250-299
300-349
350-399
400-449
450-491

LOPUNNY

Pokémon Data

Rabbit Pokémon	
TYPE	Normal
	. . .
ABILITIES	Cute Charm
	Klutz
HEIGHT	3´11˝
WEIGHT	73.4 lbs

National Pokédex No.
428

Description

When Lopunny runs, it looks like it's bouncing on air. A clean and neat Pokémon, it grooms its ears regularly. When it senses danger, it curls itself up in its ears.

Special Moves

Bounce, Defense Curl, Jump Kick, Charm

EVO LUT ION

Buneary

Lopunny

MISMAGIUS

Pokémon Data

Magical Pokémon

TYPE	Ghost
	. . .
ABILITIES	Levitate
	. . .
HEIGHT	2′11″
WEIGHT	9.7 lbs

1–
49

50–
99

100–
149

150–
199

200–
249

250–
299

300–
349

350–
399

400–
449

450–
491

Description

Its cries sound like incantations, and anyone hearing them will experience headaches or even hallucinations. It is said that Mismagius can also chant spells of happiness.

Special Moves

Lucky Chant, Psywave, Astonish

National Pokédex No.
429

EVO LUT ION

Misdreavus → Mismagius

HONCHKROW

Pokémon Data

Big Boss Pokémon	
TYPE	Dark
	Flying
ABILITIES	Insomnia
	Super Luck
HEIGHT	2´11˝
WEIGHT	60.2 lbs

National Pokédex No.
430

Description

Honchkrow forms a gang by leading a flock of Murkrow underlings. It orders Murkrow to bring it food while it spends its time primping. It's active mostly at night.

Special Moves

Night Slash, Nasty Plot, Swagger, Dark Pulse

EVO LUT ION

Murkrow

Honchkrow

GLAMEOW

Pokémon Data

Catty Pokémon

TYPE	Normal
	. . .
ABILITIES	Limber
	Own Tempo
HEIGHT	1´08˝
WEIGHT	8.6 lbs

National Pokédex No.
431

Description

Glameow's sharp gaze can cause others to fall into a lightly hypnotized state. When annoyed, it will show its claws. When feeling playful, it will purr.

Special Moves

Scratch, Growl, Hypnosis

EVO LUT ION

Glameow → Purugly

1-49
50-99
100-149
150-199
200-249
250-299
300-349
350-399
400-449
450-491

PURUGLY

Pokémon Data

Tiger Cat Pokémon

TYPE	Normal
	. . .
ABILITIES	Thick Fat
	Own Tempo
HEIGHT	3´03˝
WEIGHT	96.6 lbs

National Pokédex No.

432

Description

Purugly will barge into other Pokémon's nests and take them over. To make itself look larger and more intimidating to opponents, it cinches its waist tightly with its two tails.

Special Moves

Assist, Slash, Body Slam, Attract

EVO LUT ION

Glameow   Purugly

CHINGLING

1-
49

50-
99

100-
149

150-
199

200
249

250-
299

300-
349

350-
399

400-
449

450-
491

Pokémon Data

Bell Pokémon

TYPE	Psychic
	. . .
ABILITIES	Levitate
	. . .
HEIGHT	0´08˝
WEIGHT	1.3 lbs

National
Pokédex No.
433

Description

Chingling bounces about, making jingling sounds as it goes. It creates these sounds by vibrating a small ball at the back of its throat. It can deafen an opponent with its cries.

Special Moves

Confusion, Uproar, Growl, Astonish

EVO LUT ION

Chingling

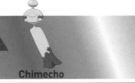
Chimecho

193

STUNKY

Pokémon Data

Skunk Pokémon

TYPE	Poison
	Dark
ABILITIES	Stench
	Aftermath
HEIGHT	1´04˝
WEIGHT	42.3 lbs

National Pokédex No.
434

Description

Stunky makes its enemies flee by spraying a horrid-smelling liquid from its rear. Once it makes contact with something, the smell will not come out for at least a day.

Special Moves

Fury Swipes, Slash, Night Slash

EVO LUT ION

Stunky   Skuntank

SKUNTANK

Pokémon Data

Skunk Pokémon	
TYPE	Poison
	Dark
ABILITIES	Stench
	Aftermath
HEIGHT	3′03″
WEIGHT	83.8 lbs

National Pokédex No.
435

Description

Skuntank can spray a stinky liquid from the tip of its tail to a distance of over 160 feet. The longer it allows the liquid to ferment within its body, the more powerful the smell.

Special Moves

Poison Gas, Memento, Flamethrower

1-49
50-99
100-149
150-199
200-249
250-299
300-349
350-399
400-449
450-491

EVO LUT ION

Stunky → Skuntank

BRONZOR

Pokémon Data

Bronze Pokémon

TYPE	Steel
	Psychic
ABILITIES	Levitate
	Heatproof
HEIGHT	1´08″
WEIGHT	133.4 lbs

National Pokédex No.
436

Description

Items similar in appearance to Bronzor have been unearthed from ancient gravesites. X-ray analyses of Bronzor's body have been conducted but were inconclusive.

Special Moves

Extrasensory, Iron Defense, Confusion

EVO LUT ION

Bronzor   Bronzong

BRONZONG

Pokémon Data

Bronze Bell Pokémon

TYPE	Steel
	Psychic
ABILITIES	Levitate
	Heatproof
HEIGHT	4´03˝
WEIGHT	412.3 lbs

National Pokédex No.
437

Description

Bronzong has the power to summon rain clouds and make them rain. Long ago, it was revered as the god of harvest. It was dug up from an ancient site after millenia.

Special Moves

Rain Dance, Gyro Ball, Future Sight

EVO LUT ION

 →

Bronzor   Bronzong

49
50-99
100-149
150-199
200-249
250-299
300-349
350-399
400-449
450-491

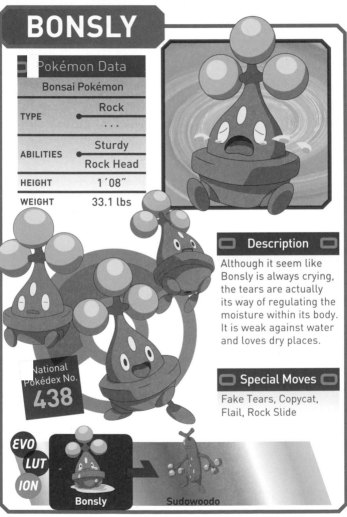

BONSLY

Pokémon Data

Bonsai Pokémon

TYPE	Rock
	. . .
ABILITIES	Sturdy
	Rock Head
HEIGHT	1′08″
WEIGHT	33.1 lbs

National Pokédex No.
438

Description

Although it seem like Bonsly is always crying, the tears are actually its way of regulating the moisture within its body. It is weak against water and loves dry places.

Special Moves

Fake Tears, Copycat, Flail, Rock Slide

EVO LUT ION

Bonsly → Sudowoodo

MIME JR.

1–
49

50–
99

100–
149

150–
199

200–
249

250–
299

300–
349

350–
399

400–
449

450–
491

Pokémon Data

Mime Pokémon	
TYPE	Psychic
	. . .
ABILITIES	Soundproof
	Filter
HEIGHT	2´00˝
WEIGHT	28.7 lbs

Description

Mime Jr. loves places where people gather. It can mimic others' movements exactly, and those being mimicked are unable to tear their eyes away.

Special Moves

Mimic, Confusion, Copycat, Role Play

National Pokédex No.
439

EVO
LUT
ION

Mime Jr.   Mr. Mime

HAPPINY

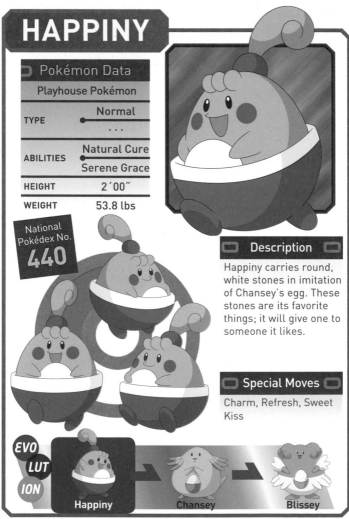

Pokémon Data

Playhouse Pokémon

TYPE	Normal
	. . .
ABILITIES	Natural Cure
	Serene Grace
HEIGHT	2´00″
WEIGHT	53.8 lbs

National Pokédex No.
440

Description

Happiny carries round, white stones in imitation of Chansey's egg. These stones are its favorite things; it will give one to someone it likes.

Special Moves

Charm, Refresh, Sweet Kiss

EVOLUTION

Happiny → Chansey → Blissey

CHATOT

Pokémon Data

Music Note Pokémon

TYPE	Normal
	Flying
ABILITIES	Keen Eye
	Tangled Feet
HEIGHT	1´08″
WEIGHT	4.2 lbs

Description

Chatot can memorize and mimic human speech. When a flock of them gather, they can all teach each other words. They flick their tail feathers back and forth in rhythm.

National Pokédex No.
441

Special Moves

Mirror Move, Chatter, Hyper Voice

EVO LUT ION

Chatot

Does not Evolve

1-49
50-99
100-149
150-199
200-249
250-299
300-349
350-399
400-449
450-491

SPIRITOMB

Pokémon Data

Forbidden Pokémon	
TYPE	Ghost
	Dark
ABILITIES	Pressure
	. . .
HEIGHT	3´03˝
WEIGHT	238.1 lbs

National Pokédex No.
442

Description

Spiritomb was born from 108 spirits coming together. They were bound to a foundation stone 500 years ago in punishment for bad deeds.

Special Moves

Confuse Ray, Shadow Sneak, Dark Pulse

EVO LUT ION

Spiritomb

Does not Evolve

GIBLE

Pokémon Data

Land Shark Pokémon

TYPE	Dragon
	Ground
ABILITIES	Sand Veil
	. . .
HEIGHT	2´04˝
WEIGHT	45.2 lbs

National Pokédex No.
443

Description

Gible lives in caves warmed by geothermal heat and shies away from the cold. If prey wanders too close to its cave, it will spring out and capture it.

Special Moves

Tackle, Sand Attack, Take Down

1-
49

50-
99

100-
149

150-
199

200-
249

250-
299

300-
349

350-
399

400-
449

450-
491

EVO
LUT
ION

Gible   Gabite   Garchomp

GABITE

Pokémon Data

	Cave Pokémon
TYPE	Dragon
	Ground
ABILITIES	Sand Veil
	...
HEIGHT	4´07″
WEIGHT	123.5 lbs

National Pokédex No.
444

Description

Because it digs up and hoards gems, Gabite´s nest is frequently targeted by thieves. It's rumored that medicine made from its scales can heal even incurable illnesses.

Special Moves

Take Down, Dragon Rage, Dragon Claw

EVO LUT ION

 Gible

 Gabite

 Garchomp

GARCHOMP

1-49

50-99

100-149

150-199

200-249

250-299

300-349

350-399

400-449

450-491

Pokémon Data

Mach Pokémon

TYPE	Dragon
	Ground
ABILITIES	Sand Veil
	. . .
HEIGHT	6´03˝
WEIGHT	209.4 lbs

National Pokédex No.
445

Description

When Garchomp flies, it contracts its body and extends its wings. When it does so, it looks almost like a jet and flies just as fast. It's almost impossible for its prey to escape.

Special Moves

Sand Tomb, Crunch, Dragon Rush

EVOLUTION

Gible → Gabite → Garchomp

205

MUNCHLAX

Pokémon Data

Big Eater Pokémon

TYPE	Normal
	. . .
ABILITIES	Pickup
	Thick Fat
HEIGHT	2´00″
WEIGHT	231.5 lbs

National Pokédex No.
446

Description

Every day Munchlax eats its body weight in food. It often hides food under its fur—but just as often, it forgets about the food that it hid.

Special Moves

Odor Sleuth, Recycle, Fling

EVO LUT ION

Munchlax   Snorlax

RIOLU

1–49
50–99
100–149
150–199
200–249
250–299
300–349
350–399
400–449
450–491

Pokémon Data

Emanation Pokémon

TYPE	Fighting . . .
ABILITIES	Steadfast Inner Focus
HEIGHT	2′04″
WEIGHT	44.5 lbs

Description

Riolu emits wave pulses from its body that let its companions know when it is scared or sad. It has a tough constitution; it is able to cross three mountains and two valleys in a single night.

National Pokédex No.
447

Special Moves

Counter, Force Palm, Feint

 EVO LUT ION

Riolu   Lucario

LUCARIO

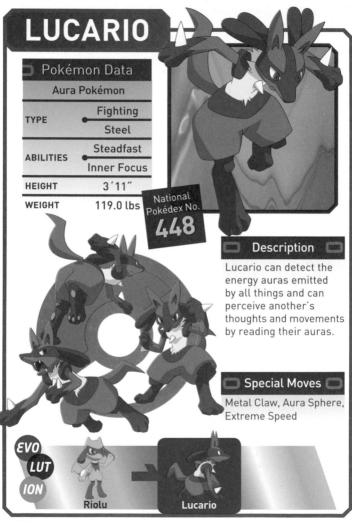

Pokémon Data

Aura Pokémon

TYPE	Fighting
	Steel
ABILITIES	Steadfast
	Inner Focus
HEIGHT	3´11˝
WEIGHT	119.0 lbs

National Pokédex No.
448

Description

Lucario can detect the energy auras emitted by all things and can perceive another's thoughts and movements by reading their auras.

Special Moves

Metal Claw, Aura Sphere, Extreme Speed

EVO LUT ION

Riolu → Lucario

HIPPOPOTAS

Pokémon Data

Hippo Pokémon	
TYPE	Ground . . .
ABILITIES	Sand Stream . . .
HEIGHT	2′07″
WEIGHT	109.1 lbs

1-49

50-99

100-149

150-199

200-249

250-299

300-349

350-399

400-449

450-491

National Pokédex No.
449

Description

Hippopotas likes to live in arid lands and does not like getting wet. In order to protect its body it secretes sand, not sweat.

Special Moves

Bite, Yawn, Take Down, Sand Tomb

EVO LUT ION

Hippopotas

Hippowdon

HIPPOWDON

Pokémon Data

Heavyweight Pokémon

TYPE	Ground ...
ABILITIES	Sand Stream ...
HEIGHT	6′07″
WEIGHT	661.4 lbs

National Pokédex No.
450

Description

Hippowdon can create tornados by blasting sand out of the holes in its body. It has a huge mouth, which it can stretch open almost seven feet wide.

Special Moves

Crunch, Earthquake, Double-Edge

EVOLUTION

Hippopotas

Hippowdon

SKORUPI

Pokémon Data

Scorpion Pokémon

TYPE	Poison
	Bug
ABILITIES	Battle Armor
	Sniper
HEIGHT	2'07"
WEIGHT	26.5 lbs

National Pokédex No.
451

Description

Skorupi lives in dry areas. It holds its prey using the claw on its trail and then injects a poison with its stingers. It will not let go until the poison has taken effect.

Special Moves

Poison Sting, Leer, Pin Missile

EVO LUT ION

Skorupi

Drapion

1-49
50-99
100-149
150-199
200-249
250-299
300-349
350-399
400-449
450-491

DRAPION

Pokémon Data

Ogre Scorp Pokémon

TYPE	Poison
	Dark
ABILITIES	Battle Armor
	Sniper
HEIGHT	4′03″
WEIGHT	135.6 lbs

National Pokédex No.

452

Description

A hard armor covers Drapion's entire body. Its head can rotate 180°, so it has no blind spot. Its claws have enormous destructive power and their tips are poisonous.

Special Moves

Toxic Spikes, Poison Fang, Cross Poison

EVO LUT ION

Skorupi → Drapion

CROAGUNK

Pokémon Data

Toxic Mouth Pokémon

TYPE	Poison
	Fighting
ABILITIES	Anticipation
	Dry Skin
HEIGHT	2´04"
WEIGHT	50.7 lbs

National Pokédex No.
453

Description

Just before Croagunk attacks it puffs out the poison pouches in its cheeks and makes a croaking noise. Waiting for just the right moment, it will spring at its opponent.

Special Moves

Taunt, Poison Jab, Feint Attack, Revenge

EVO LUT ION

Croagunk ➤ Toxicroak

1–49
50–99
100–149
150–199
200–249
250–299
300–349
350–399
400–449
450–491

TOXICROAK

Pokémon Data

Toxic Mouth Pokémon

TYPE	Poison
	Fighting
ABILITIES	Anticipation
	Dry Skin
HEIGHT	4′03″
WEIGHT	97.9 lbs

National Pokédex No.
454

Description

The spikes on Toxicroak's knuckles are infused with a poison created in its poison pouch. This poison is so powerful that even a little scratch can be fatal.

Special Moves

Sucker Punch, Poison Jab, Sludge Bomb

EVO LUT ION

Croagunk

Toxicroak

CARNIVINE

Pokémon Data

Bug Catcher Pokémon

TYPE	Grass …
ABILITIES	Levitate …
HEIGHT	4´07˝
WEIGHT	59.5 lbs

1–
50-99
100-149
150-199
200-249
250-299
300-349
350-399
400-449
450-491

Description

Carnivine lures in its prey with the sweet scent of its saliva, then swallows the prey whole. Carnivine takes one whole day to digest its food.

National Pokédex No.
455

Special Moves

Sweet Scent, Crunch, Power Whip

EVO LUT ION

Carnivine — Does not Evolve

215

FINNEON

Pokémon Data

Wing Fish Pokémon

TYPE	Water
	. . .
ABILITIES	Swift Swim
	Storm Drain
HEIGHT	1´04″
WEIGHT	15.4 lbs

Description

As darkness descends, the patterns on its tail shine brightly. The more it basks in the sun's warm light, the brighter the colors. Finneon is also known as the "Beautifly of the Sea."

National Pokédex No.

456

Special Moves

Water Gun, Attract, Water Pulse

EVO LUT ION

Finneon → Lumineon

LUMINEON

Pokémon Data

Neon Pokémon

TYPE	Water
	...
ABILITIES	Swift Swim
	Storm Drain
HEIGHT	3'11"
WEIGHT	52.9 lbs

1-49
50-99
100-149
150-199
200-249
250-299
300-349
350-399
400-449
450-491

Description

Lumineon lives at the bottom of the ocean. It attracts prey with the shimmering patterns on its four top fins.

National Pokédex No.

457

Special Moves

Safeguard, Aqua Ring, Whirlpool

EVO LUT ION

Finneon → Lumineon

217

MANTYKE

Pokémon Data

Kite Pokémon

TYPE	Water
	Flying
ABILITIES	Swift Swim
	Water Absorb
HEIGHT	3´03˝
WEIGHT	143.3 lbs

National Pokédex No. 458

Description

Mantyke becomes very attached to humans. Using its two horns, it can sense even slight movements by changes in water pressure.

Special Moves

Bubble Beam, Wing Attack, Take Down

EVOLUTION

Mantyke → Mantine

SNOVER

1-49
50-99
100-149
150-199
200-249
250-299
300-349
350-399
400-449
450-491

Pokémon Data

Frost Tree Pokémon

TYPE	Grass
	Ice
ABILITIES	Snow Warning
	. . .
HEIGHT	3'03"
WEIGHT	111.3 lbs

National Pokédex No.
459

Description

Snover lives on snow-capped mountains. If humans approach, it will come up to them out of curiosity. In the spring, berries grow in a ring around its middle, like a belt of frozen treats.

Special Moves

Ice Shard, Razor Leaf, Icy Wind

EVO LUT ION

Snover   Abomasnow

219

ABOMASNOW

Pokémon Data

Frost Tree Pokémon

TYPE	Grass
	Ice
ABILITIES	Snow Warning
	. . .
HEIGHT	7´03˝
WEIGHT	298.7 lbs

National Pokédex No.

460

Description

Abomasnow can create blizzards and lives on mountains that are covered in snow year-round. Some speculate that the Abominable Snowman might actually be Abomasnow.

Special Moves

Wood Hammer, Blizzard, Sheer Cold

 EVO LUT ION

Snover

Abomasnow

220

WEAVILE

1-49
50-99
100-149
150-199
200-249
250-299
300-349
350-399
400-449
450-491

Pokémon Data

Sharp Claw Pokémon

TYPE	Dark
	Ice
ABILITIES	Pressure
	. . .
HEIGHT	3´07˝
WEIGHT	75.0 lbs

National Pokédex No.
461

Description

Weavile live in cold regions and hunt prey together in groups of four or five. They communicate with other each by carving mysterious symbols into trees and ice.

Special Moves

Quick Attack, Icy Wind, Night Slash, Metal Claw

EVO LUT ION

Sneasel

Weavile

MAGNEZONE

Pokémon Data

Magnet Area Pokémon

TYPE	Electric
	Steel
ABILITIES	Magnet Pull
	Sturdy
HEIGHT	3′11″
WEIGHT	396.8 lbs

National Pokédex No.
462

Description

Magnezone is the Evolved form of a Magneton after it has been exposed to a special energy field. It can blast magnetic power from all three of its units.

Special Moves

Mirror Shot, Magnet Rise, Gyro Ball, Zap Cannon

EVO LUT ION

Magnemite → Magneton → **Magnezone**

LICKILICKY

Pokémon Data

Licking Pokémon

TYPE	Normal
	. . .
ABILITIES	Own Tempo
	Oblivious
HEIGHT	5´07˝
WEIGHT	308.6 lbs

National Pokédex No.
463

Description

Lickilicky will wrap its prehensile tongue around anything in its vicinity. Getting close to it carries the risk of getting slimed with its saliva.

Special Moves

Stomp, Power Whip, Slam, Lick

EVO LUT ION

Lickitung → Lickilicky

1-49
50-99
100-149
150-199
200-249
250-299
300-349
350-399
400-449
450-491

RHYPERIOR

Pokémon Data

Drill Pokémon

TYPE	Ground
	Rock
ABILITIES	Lightning Rod
	Solid Rock
HEIGHT	7´10˝
WEIGHT	623.5 lbs

National Pokédex No.
464

Description

Rhyperior stuffs rocks into the holes in its hands and shoots them out using its muscles. It's been known on occasion to shoot Geodude in this way.

Special Moves

Hammer Arm, Earthquake, Horn Drill, Rock Wrecker

EVO LUT ION

Rhyhorn

Rhydon

Rhyperior

TANGROWTH

Pokémon Data

Vine Pokémon

TYPE	Grass
	. . .
ABILITIES	Chlorophyll
	Leaf Guard
HEIGHT	6´07˝
WEIGHT	283.5 lbs

National Pokédex No.
465

Description

Tangrowth grasps and captures its prey by extending its long arms, which are actually thick bundles of plant vines. If some of these vines are ripped off, it can regrow them.

Special Moves

Ancient Power, Tickle, Wring Out, Power Whip

EVO LUT ION

Tangela → Tangrowth

1–49
50–99
100–149
150–199
200–249
250–299
300–349
350–399
400–449
450–491

ELECTIVIRE

Pokémon Data

Thunderbolt Pokémon

TYPE	Electric
	...
ABILITIES	Motor Drive
	...
HEIGHT	5′11″
WEIGHT	305.6 lbs

National Pokédex No.
466

Description

Electivire attacks by pressing the tips of its two tails against its opponent and releasing a massive jolt of 20,000 volts of electricity.

Special Moves

Thunderbolt, Thunder, Giga Impact

EVO LUT ION

Elekid → Electabuzz → Electivire

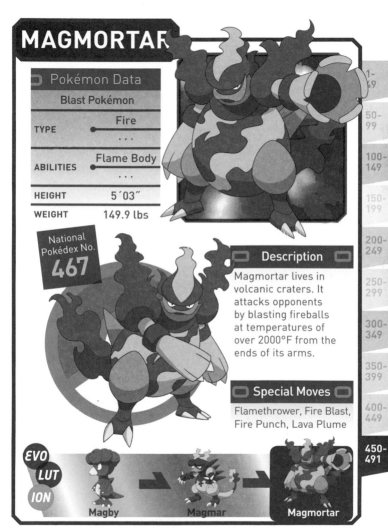

MAGMORTAR

Pokémon Data

Blast Pokémon

TYPE	Fire ...
ABILITIES	Flame Body ...
HEIGHT	5'03"
WEIGHT	149.9 lbs

National Pokédex No. **467**

Description

Magmortar lives in volcanic craters. It attacks opponents by blasting fireballs at temperatures of over 2000°F from the ends of its arms.

Special Moves

Flamethrower, Fire Blast, Fire Punch, Lava Plume

EVOLUTION

Magby → Magmar → Magmortar

1-49
50-99
100-149
150-199
200-249
250-299
300-349
350-399
400-449
450-491

TOGEKISS

Pokémon Data

Jubilee Pokémon

TYPE	Normal
	Flying
ABILITIES	Hustle
	Serene Grace
HEIGHT	4′11″
WEIGHT	83.8 lbs

National Pokédex No.
468

Description

Togekiss never appears in regions that are experiencing strife. Recently, sightings of it have become extremely rare, perhaps because the amount of conflicts has increased.

Special Moves

Sky Attack, Aura Sphere, Extreme Speed, Air Slash

EVO LUT ION

Togepi → Togetic → **Togekiss**

YANMEGA

1-49
50-99
100-149
150-199
200-249
250-299
300-349
350-399
400-449
450-491

Pokémon Data

Ogre Darner Pokémon	
TYPE	Bug
	Flying
ABILITIES	Speed Boost
	Tinted Lens
HEIGHT	6′03″
WEIGHT	113.5 lbs

National Pokédex No.
469

Description

Yanmega attacks using shockwaves created by the beating of its wings. These shockwaves cause an opponent's insides to vibrate, resulting in internal damage.

Special Moves

Slash, Ancient Power, Air Slash, Bug Buzz

EVO LUT ION

Yanma → Yanmega

LEAFEON

Pokémon Data

Verdant Pokémon

TYPE	Grass
	...
ABILITIES	Leaf Guard
	...
HEIGHT	3'03"
WEIGHT	56.2 lbs

National Pokédex No.
470

Description

Leafeon is one Evolved form of an Eevee. Just like a plant, it creates oxygen by basking in sunlight. Because of this, it is always surrounded by clean, pure air.

Special Moves

Giga Drain, Grass Whistle, Leaf Blade

EVO LUT ION

 Eevee → Leafeon

GLACEON

1-49
50-99
100-149
150-199
200-249
250-299
300-349
350-399
400-449
450-491

Pokémon Data

Fresh Snow Pokémon

TYPE	Ice
	...
ABILITIES	Snow Cloak
	...
HEIGHT	2'07"
WEIGHT	57.1 lbs

National Pokédex No.
471

Description

As a defense measure, Glaceon can freeze all the fur on its body. Every single frozen hair becomes as sharp as a needle.

Special Moves

Quick Attack, Ice Fang, Mirror Coat, Hail

EVO LUT ION

Eevee → Glaceon

231

GLISCOR

Pokémon Data

Fang Scorpion Pokémon

TYPE	
	Ground
	Flying

ABILITIES	
	Hyper Cutter
	Sand Veil

HEIGHT	6´07″
WEIGHT	93.7 lbs

Description

Gliscor uses its tail to hang from tree branches and waits for prey to walk below it. If it sees that the prey is not on guard, it swoops down from above to attack.

National Pokédex No.
472

Special Moves

Screech, X-Scissor, Guillotine

EVO LUT ION

Gligar → Gliscor

MAMOSWINE

Pokémon Data

Twin Tusk Pokémon	
TYPE	Ice
	Ground
ABILITIES	Oblivious
	Snow Cloak
HEIGHT	8'02"
WEIGHT	641.5 lbs

National Pokédex No.
473

1-49

50-99

100-149

150-199

200-249

250-299

300-349

350-399

400-449

450-491

Description

Mamoswine's two huge tusks are made of ice. Their numbers have decreased greatly since the last ice age ended and the world's temperature rose.

Special Moves

Earthquake, Take Down, Ancient Power

EVOLUTION

Swinub

Piloswine

Mamoswine

233

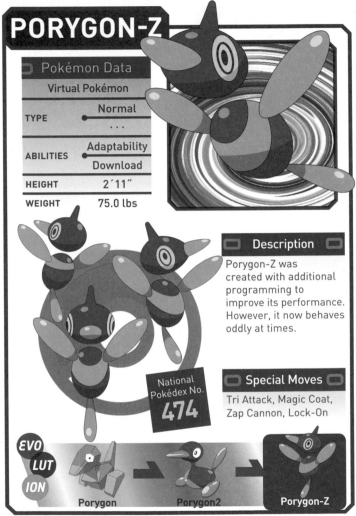

PORYGON-Z

Pokémon Data

Virtual Pokémon

TYPE	Normal
	...
ABILITIES	Adaptability
	Download
HEIGHT	2´11˝
WEIGHT	75.0 lbs

Description

Porygon-Z was created with additional programming to improve its performance. However, it now behaves oddly at times.

National Pokédex No.
474

Special Moves

Tri Attack, Magic Coat, Zap Cannon, Lock-On

EVOLUTION

Porygon ▸ Porygon2 ▸ Porygon-Z

GALLADE

1–
49

50–
99

100–
149

150–
199

200–
249

250–
299

300–
349

350–
399

400–
449

450–
491

Pokémon Data

Blade Pokémon

TYPE	Psychic
	Fighting
ABILITIES	Steadfast
	. . .
HEIGHT	5′03″
WEIGHT	114.6 lbs

National
Pokédex No.
475

Description

A very polite Pokémon, Gallade fights using elbow blades that it can extend and retract at will. It is a master of *Iai* (the art of drawing a sword).

Special Moves

Fury Cutter, Swords Dance, Psycho Cut

EVO LUT ION

Ralts ➤ Kirlia ➤ Gallade

PROBOPASS

Pokémon Data

Compass Pokémon

TYPE	Rock
	Steel
ABILITIES	Sturdy
	Magnet Pull
HEIGHT	4´07˝
WEIGHT	749.6 lbs

National Pokédex No.
476

Description

Probopass emits a strong magnetic force from its entire body. It can also manipulate its three smaller units, the Mini-Noses.

Special Moves

Iron Defense, Magnet Bomb, Stone Edge

EVO LUT ION

Nosepass

Probopass

DUSKNOIR

Pokémon Data

Gripper Pokémon

TYPE	Ghost
	...
ABILITIES	Pressure
	...
HEIGHT	7′03″
WEIGHT	235.0 lbs

1-
49

50-
99

100-
149

150-
199

200-
249

250-
299

300-
349

350-
399

400-
449

450-
491

Description

Dusknoir uses the disc on its head to receive radio waves from the spirit world. It is rumored that these convey commands to take people away to the spirit world.

Special Moves

Shadow Punch, Curse, Shadow Sneak

National Pokédex No.
477

EVOLUTION

Duskull

Dusclops

Dusknoir

FROSLASS

Pokémon Data

Snow Land Pokémon

TYPE	Ice
	Ghost
ABILITIES	Snow Cloak
	. . .
HEIGHT	4´03″
WEIGHT	58.6 lbs

National Pokédex No.
478

Description

The cold air that it breathes out is at an unbelievable -60ºF. Anything that Froslass breathes upon will soon freeze. What seems to be its body is actually a hollow cavity.

Special Moves

Icy Wind, Ominous Wind, Ice Shard, Blizzard

EVO LUT ION

Snorunt → Froslass

ROTOM

1-49
50-99
100-149
150-199
200-249
250-299
300-349
350-399
400-449
450-491

Pokémon Data

Plasma Pokémon

TYPE	Electric
	Ghost
ABILITIES	Levitate
	. . .
HEIGHT	1´00˝
WEIGHT	0.7 lbs

National Pokédex No. **479**

Description

A Rotom's body is made of plasma. They are known to burrow into electric appliances such as televisions and toasters and make them malfunction.

Special Moves

Shock Wave, Ominous Wind, Substitute

EVO LUT ION

Rotom

Does not Evolve

239

UXIE

Pokémon Data

Knowledge Pokémon	
TYPE	Psychic
	...
ABILITIES	Levitate
	...
HEIGHT	1´00˝
WEIGHT	0.7 lbs

National Pokédex No.
480

Description

Known as the "Being of Knowledge," Uxie brought about the birth of intelligence in human life. It's rumored to have the power to erase memories.

Special Moves

Yawn, Future Sight, Rest, Extrasensory

EVOLUTION

Uxie

Does not Evolve

MESPRIT

Pokémon Data

Emotion Pokémon

TYPE	Psychic . . .
ABILITIES	Levitate Snow Cloak
HEIGHT	1´00˝
WEIGHT	0.7 lbs

National Pokédex No.
481

Description

Known as the "Being of Emotion," Mesprit taught humanity the nobility of sorrow, pain and joy. It sleeps at the bottom of a lake, but at times its soul slips out of its physical body to fly.

Special Moves

Lucky Chant, Future Sight, Healing Wish

EVO LUT ION

Mesprit

Does not Evolve

1-49
50-99
100-149
150-199
200-249
250-299
300-349
350-399
400-449
450-491

AZELF

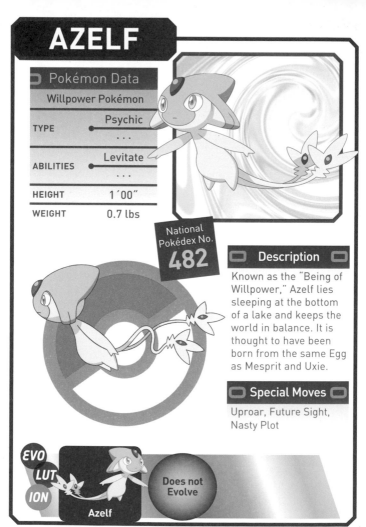

Pokémon Data

Willpower Pokémon

TYPE	Psychic
	...
ABILITIES	Levitate
	...
HEIGHT	1´00˝
WEIGHT	0.7 lbs

National
Pokédex No.
482

Description

Known as the "Being of Willpower," Azelf lies sleeping at the bottom of a lake and keeps the world in balance. It is thought to have been born from the same Egg as Mesprit and Uxie.

Special Moves

Uproar, Future Sight, Nasty Plot

EVO LUT ION

Azelf

Does not Evolve

242

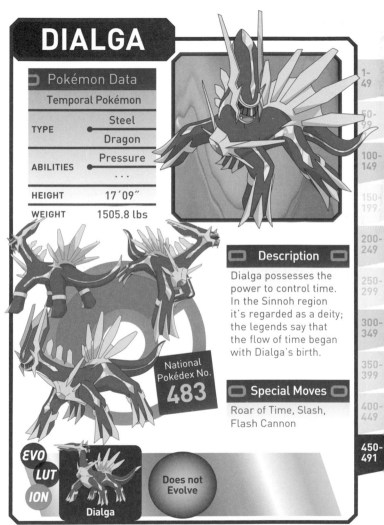

DIALGA

Pokémon Data

Temporal Pokémon

TYPE	Steel
	Dragon
ABILITIES	Pressure
	. . .
HEIGHT	17´09˝
WEIGHT	1505.8 lbs

National Pokédex No.
483

Description

Dialga possesses the power to control time. In the Sinnoh region it's regarded as a deity; the legends say that the flow of time began with Dialga's birth.

Special Moves

Roar of Time, Slash, Flash Cannon

EVO LUT ION

Dialga

Does not Evolve

1-49
50-99
100-149
150-199
200-249
250-299
300-349
350-399
400-449
450-491

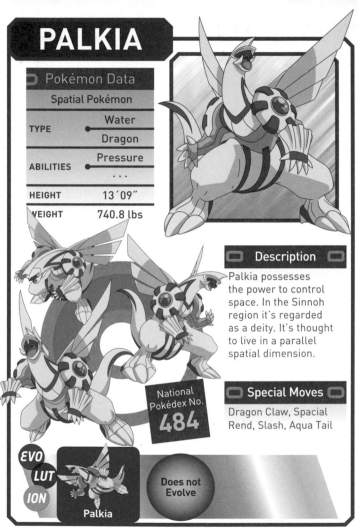

PALKIA

Pokémon Data

Spatial Pokémon

TYPE	Water
	Dragon
ABILITIES	Pressure
	. . .
HEIGHT	13´09˝
WEIGHT	740.8 lbs

Description

Palkia possesses the power to control space. In the Sinnoh region it's regarded as a deity. It's thought to live in a parallel spatial dimension.

National Pokédex No.
484

Special Moves

Dragon Claw, Spacial Rend, Slash, Aqua Tail

EVO LUT ION

Palkia

Does not Evolve

HEATRAN

1-
49

50-
99

100-
49

150-
199

200-
249

250-
299

300-
349

350-
399

400-
449

450-
491

Pokémon Data

Lava Dome Pokémon

TYPE	Fire
	Steel
ABILITIES	Flash Fire
	. . .
HEIGHT	5′07″
WEIGHT	948.0 lbs

National
Pokédex No.
485

Description

Heatran lives in
volcanic caves. It can
crawl about the walls
and ceilings using its
cross-shaped claws.

Special Moves

Crunch, Earth Power,
Heat Wave

EVO LUT ION

Heatran

Does not
Evolve

REGIGIGAS

Pokémon Data

Colossal Pokémon

TYPE	Normal
	. . .
ABILITIES	Slow Start
	. . .
HEIGHT	12´02˝
WEIGHT	925.9 lbs

National Pokédex No.
486

Description

One legend states that Regigigas once towed an entire continent. It is very slow when it first starts moving.

Special Moves

Superpower, Crush Grip, Zen Headbutt

EVOLUTION

Regigigas

Does not Evolve

GIRATINA

Pokémon Data

Renegade Pokémon

TYPE	Ghost
	Dragon
ABILITIES	Pressure
	. . .
HEIGHT	14´09˝
WEIGHT	1653.5 lbs

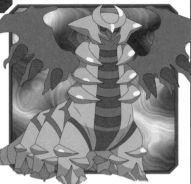

National Pokédex No.
487

Description

Giratina is a Pokémon that appeared at an ancient gravesite. It's said to inhabit a nether dimension.

Special Moves

Dragon Breath, Shadow Force, Shadow Claw

EVO LUT ION

Giratina

Does not Evolve

1-9
50-99
100-149
150-199
200-249
250-299
300-349
350-399
400-449
450-491

CRESSELIA

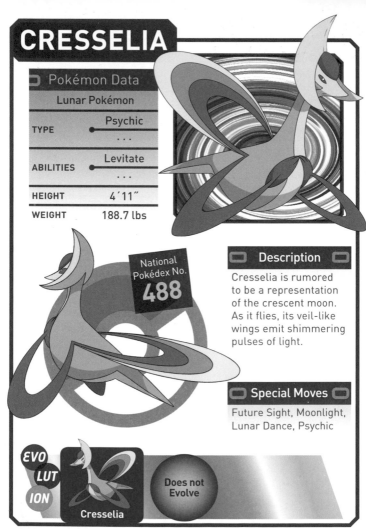

Pokémon Data

Lunar Pokémon

TYPE	Psychic
	. . .
ABILITIES	Levitate
	. . .
HEIGHT	4´11˝
WEIGHT	188.7 lbs

National Pokédex No.
488

Description

Cresselia is rumored to be a representation of the crescent moon. As it flies, its veil-like wings emit shimmering pulses of light.

Special Moves

Future Sight, Moonlight, Lunar Dance, Psychic

EVOLUTION

Cresselia

Does not Evolve

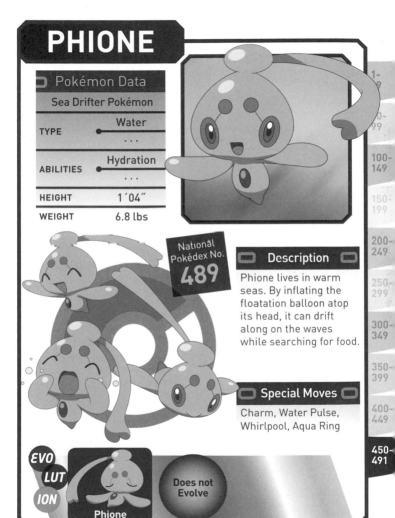

PHONE

Pokémon Data

Sea Drifter Pokémon

TYPE	Water
	...
ABILITIES	Hydration
	...
HEIGHT	1´04"
WEIGHT	6.8 lbs

National Pokédex No.

489

Description

Phione lives in warm seas. By inflating the floatation balloon atop its head, it can drift along on the waves while searching for food.

Special Moves

Charm, Water Pulse, Whirlpool, Aqua Ring

EVO LUT ION

Phione — Does not Evolve

1-9
10-99
100-149
150-199
200-249
250-299
300-349
350-399
400-449
450-491

MANAPHY

Pokémon Data

Seafaring Pokémon

TYPE	Water ...
ABILITIES	Hydration ...
HEIGHT	1´00˝
WEIGHT	3.1 lbs

National Pokédex No.
490

Description

Manaphy's body is made of 80 percent water. It will swim great distances to return to the cold sea where it was born. It is easily influenced by its environment.

Special Moves

Water Pulse, Dive, Heart Swap

EVOLUTION

Manaphy — Does not Evolve

DARKRAI

Pokémon Data

Pitch-Black Pokémon

TYPE	Dark
	...

ABILITIES	Bad Dreams
	...

HEIGHT	4'11"
WEIGHT	111.3 lbs

Description

Appearing on the night of a new moon, Darkai has the dangerous power to put humans to sleep and force them to dream.

National Pokédex No.
491

Special Moves

Hypnosis, Dark Void, Dream Eater

EVO LUT ION

Darkrai

Does not Evolve

1-49
50-99
100-149
150-199
200-249
250-299
300-349
350-399
400-449
450-491